Round Trip

LOUISE TURNER & WANDA JENNINGS

BOOK SIX OF THE MAGNOLIA MANOR SERIES

Printed in the United States of America
First Printed February 2022
Cover Art by Victoria L. Hawkins

Large Print Edition Published July 2022

Published by:

Southern Willow Publishing, LLC
1114 Highway 96,
Suite C-1, #340
Kathleen, Georgia 31047

ISBN: 978-1-956544-14-5

This book is dedicated to the talented performers on stages across the country, as well as the crew members and those who work tirelessly to bring us all live theatre. We hope this book brings you some of the joy that you have all brought us over the years.

∽Chapter One∽

The sun shone in brightly through the blinds in the cafe. Opal Tyler, Ruby Montgomery, and Maude Cooper walked around the groups of people to a small table near the wide counter that was full of hungry customers. The Starlight Cafe had done well since they opened a little over two years ago, and was a favorite lunch spot for most of the people in Rhinestone. Travelers far and wide stopped in for their signature homemade pies and foot long hotdogs.

"I'd rather sit in a booth, but this will be fine," Maude sighed.

"We didn't beat the lunch crowd today," Opal shrugged.

"I need a vacation," Maude yawned. She sat down in the metal chair and stretched her arms over her head.

"The usual?" Donny, the owner, asked them.

They all nodded and Maude added, "Donny, two slices of pie please."

Donny smiled and said he'd have it all ready as soon as possible.

"I'm already packed. I've been waiting for this trip for two years," Maude chirped.

"It's Thursday afternoon. We don't leave til Sunday morning," Opal laughed.

"You can never be too prepared," Maude said. "There's so much to do before we leave."

"That's the truth," Ruby added. "We've got to get through this school talent show first of all. Mavis has been fretting all week about this talent show tomorrow night. She's been practicing nonstop."

"Rehearsing," Opal corrected her.

"Right," Ruby nodded. "Rehearsing. She's been over at Nadine's twice a week for the past month taking voice lessons."

Maude rolled her eyes and sighed audibly. "We were having such a nice time."

"What are you talking about?" Ruby asked.

"You just had to go and mention her name," Maude sulked.

"Nadine?" Ruby asked.

Maude groaned loudly and mimed puking into her handbag.

"Well, that's exactly why I didn't mention it before now. Anyway, I thought y'all were in a good place," Ruby said.

"We were, til she had to go and start it all up again," Maude grumbled.

"What do you mean?" Ruby asked.

"She near about killed me," Maude said dramatically. "Right in the middle of Opal's shop. She's nothing but an old bully. Practically beat me up."

Opal shook her head and interjected," That's not exactly how it happened."

"Whose side are you on?" Maude asked.

"I don't take sides," Opal smiled. "Just call me Switzerland."

"What happened now?" Ruby asked. "Or do I even want to know?"

"Oh, she's just sour that Nadine beat her in that radio contest last week. They were both in the salon and both near about jumped over the front counter to get to the telephone. Maude tried to scale the counter like she was Bo Duke or something," Opal explained.

Ruby hid her laughter behind her napkin. "What kind of contest was this?"

"You had to be the tenth caller and Nadine got to the phone first," Opal finished.

"She pushed me out of the way!" Maude snapped. "I had my hand on the darn thing!"

"Well, I don't know about that," Opal said. "You were both elbowing each other and near about barreled poor Ms. Robinson over in the process."

"She was trying to get to the phone, too," Maude said.

"No she wasn't," Opal shook her head. "She barely knows who she is anymore, let alone how to use a telephone. Y'all had to go and make a scene in front of her and half the town. Y'all should be embarrassed."

Maude crossed her arms and glared at Opal. "Nadine was already done with her appointment. She was waiting around just so she could pull one over on me. I'd been talking about that contest all week."

"You were done, too," Opal pointed out. "You had plenty of time to make it back to your house to sit by your own phone instead of tying up my shop's line."

"Y'all are too grown for this," Ruby said adamantly. "Things were going so well. This one little radio contest isn't worth it."

Before Opal could pipe up again, Maude shushed her.

"What in the world?" Ruby asked.

"Opal Tyler, don't you dare!" Maude said.

"What did you do?" Ruby turned to Maude.

"She ordered fertilizer for Nadine's entire front yard last month," Opal squeaked. "When Nadine was in Atlanta visiting her sister that weekend."

"What?" Ruby gasped.

"Well, her front yard was looking dry. It hasn't rained hardly all spring," Maude explained.

"You had them spread a layer of manure across her whole yard," Opal retorted.

"They brought in a sprayer and wet it down real nice," Maude added.

"Maude! That's awful!" Ruby sighed. "Last month? I hadn't heard about this!"

"Her yard has never looked better," Maude smiled.

"Smelled like a bunch of chicken houses on fire," Opal coughed. "She had to have been fit to be tied when she got home."

"I can imagine so," Ruby shook her head. "What did she say when she got home?"

"Nothing," Maude said.

"Nothing?" Ruby asked.

"Took the wind right out of Maude's sails," Opal laughed. "Nadine never said a word to anyone about it. Maude waited all afternoon to see her reaction, but Nadine just walked inside and acted like everything was normal."

"She's so rude like that," Maude grumbled.

"That was so rude of you, Maude," Ruby said.

"She had a herd of chickens sent to my house before that!" Maude barked.

"A herd?" Opal asked.

"Well, whatever you call them," Maude said. "Thirteen chickens crated on my porch."

"She just knows you love fried chicken," Ruby said.

"Ruby, no!" Opal gasped. "They're rescue chickens. I got to them before this one could ring their necks. Thank God Mortie helped me find a good chicken coop for them over in Junction at the feed store. They're too cute to eat. Leroy already eats out of my hand when I let them out every morning."

"I thought they were all hens?" Ruby wondered.

"They are," Opal nodded. "Leroy, Petunia, Ellis, Frankie, Jasmine, Clara, Belle, Naydina, Little Maude, Rue, Winnie, Lulu, and Pepper."

"Such interesting names," Ruby smiled.

"Can you believe she named a darned chicken after me?" Maude asked Ruby.

"Two of them actually. Winnie is short for Winifred. They're the two that get their feathers ruffled the easiest," Opal explained. "Rue is short for Ruby. She's the nicest."

"That's so sweet!" Ruby exclaimed.

"See! Opal made pets of them before I could even think about cooking them," Maude sighed. "I doubt that was Nadine's intention anyway."

"Well, you did call into that QVC program and sign her up for the lifetime supply of dental floss. And you signed her up for Meals on Wheels last Christmas," Opal reminded her.

"Just looking out for her," Maude shrugged.

"You just can't help yourself, can you?" sighed Ruby. "I swear! She was instrumental in saving all of our lives a few years ago and y'all have already sunk back into your level of depravity!"

"She makes my life miserable," Maude interjected, but Ruby put her hand up to stop her.

"Don't start pouting now," Opal chided Maude. "I think Sarah's bringing over your food."

At the news of food, Maude perked up instantly.

"See, she brought your food first like a toddler," Ruby sassed.

"Here you are, Maude," Sarah smiled. She set the hot platter that carried a large cheeseburger, fries, and a stack of onion rings down in front of Maude. "And here's your slices of pie."

"Looks heavenly," Maude grinned. Her mouth was practically watering at the sight of the meal.

"And here is your BLT, Opal, minus the B. And your turkey club, Ruby," Donny said. He was standing behind his wife, Sarah, who quickly scooted out of the way.

"Wonderful!" exclaimed Ruby. "Thank you both. If you get a minute, come sit down with us."

"It was good seeing y'all," Sarah smiled. "But I've got to head on up to the school to help set up for the talent show tomorrow night. I got roped into helping set up and decorate the stage."

"Jameson's there right now. He and Mitch built the podium last night and the woodshop class at the high school was going to paint it this morning," Ruby nodded.

"I'm excited to see the show, but I can only take so much of the constant noise coming down the stairs every afternoon and evening," Sarah laughed.

Ruby smiled and nodded along. "Mavis is about to drive us all crazy with her excitement, too."

"I think every girl in the elementary school signed up for the show," Donny added. "Mona's singing a little song she made up about her mama's apple pie. Couldn't bribe Harry to get up onstage. He's such a quiet young man."

"He's got the right idea," Maude chimed in. Bits of beef and cheese flew out of her mouth as she spoke.

"Such a lady," Opal sighed.

"Well, I'll see y'all tomorrow evening at the school," Sarah smiled.

Ruby, Opal, and Maude thanked them again and went back to their plates.

"I love this little place," Opal beamed. She bit into her sandwich and relished the taste. Donny always made the best BLT, minus the bacon, just for her. The toasted bread, extra mayonnaise, crisp lettuce, and juicy tomato was like heaven on a plate.

"Less than seventy-two hours until I'm in New York City. If I could leave now, I would," Maude said earnestly.

"It's going to be grand," Ruby agreed.

"What are the names of the museums you wanted to go to again?" Maude asked after they had finished their meal.

"The Metropolitan Museum of Art," Opal smiled. "The Met. It sounds so fancy. Ricky said it is the pinnacle of class."

Maude rolled her eyes, but wrote it down on the piece of paper she had fished out of her purse.

"Did the airline say how many bags we could bring?" Ruby asked.

"How many do you intend on bringing?" Opal asked.

"Enough to get the job done," Ruby shrugged. "There's all kinds of treasures I might need to bring back."

"You can't bring those back, Ruby," Opal scolded. "They belong to the museum."

"I wasn't going to steal anything," Ruby gasped. "I was talking about the giftshops and stores."

"They'll stop you in a heartbeat if they think you're trying to smuggle something in or out," Opal continued.

"You would know!" retorted Maude. She still had not forgiven Opal for what had transpired on their first major trip in the sixties when Opal accidentally, her words, caused Maude to get momentarily detained in the airport when Opal had smuggled in Leo, her prized rescue kitten she had catnapped in Italy, in her carry-on bag.

Opal ignored Maude's outburst and grinned at Ruby. "It'll be like nothing you've ever seen before," Opal assured her. "The street vendors alone will have a field day with you. You've never seen so many purses and outfits, jewelry and trinkets. Never ending options. Speaking of which, don't disappear behind any curtains or get lost in any rooms. We stick together."

"Opal's right. We ain't about to get kidnapped," Maude agreed.

"Who would want to kidnap a bunch of fifty-year-old bitties?" Ruby laughed.

"I meant we stick together or else Jameson will kill us after he sees what Ruby brings back," Opal laughed. "The kidnappers would bring you two back in a heartbeat anyway. Maude, because you stay grumpy, and Ruby because you'd ask a lot of questions."

Maude mumbled something under her breath and ate her second piece of pie.

"Jameson did say no more Elvis art collections," Ruby chuckled. "He put the velvet piece in the trailer because he said he was tired of it nearly giving him a heart attack when he walked by it at night."

For Ruby's fiftieth birthday last September, Jameson had gifted her a small trailer, outfitted with a full kitchen, cozy living room, and two bonus rooms that she had quickly turned into a guest room and storage area. She named it the Shangri-La after the hotel the three friends had stayed in during their surprise visit to Nepal nearly thirty years ago. When her parents or brother and his family came to visit, they had the perfect place to stay that offered privacy and quiet.

Jameson was an excellent gift giver. The trailer was easily her second favorite gift from him, narrowly missing out on first place to the floor to ceiling aquarium he had gifted her for Christmas a few years back.

"I'm sure we'll find all kinds of things to deck the Shangri-La in," Opal said. "And we'll have to get everyone updated shirts of course."

"Of course," Ruby agreed.

"Are you about done?" Opal asked Maude. "Or do we need to order you a third piece of pie?"

"I think I'm done, at least for now," Maude said. She had already licked the plate clean from the two pieces of chocolate pie with extra whip cream.

"I'm going to run by the Piggly Wiggly for some chicken before I pick up the kids from school. Then I've got to get Mavis over to Nadine's for one last rehearsal tonight. I'll see y'all tomorrow evening at six o'clock. Then we'll all go out to eat afterwards. I know Mavis will be starving after putting on a show," Ruby nodded.

"I can't wait to hear that little angel sing," Opal smiled.

As they stood up to gather their purses, the door behind them chimed.

"Oh, hello Nadine," Opal called out loudly.

"What? Are you serious?" Maude gasped. She turned to look behind her, and sure enough, Nadine Waters had entered the Starlight Cafe wearing a tight black dress, black heels, and wide framed sunglasses.

"Mother of God! It's like you summoned her or something," Maude growled. She sank back down in her chair to hide.

"Nadine! How are you?" Opal called out.

Nadine waltzed over to their table and smiled brightly. "Good afternoon Ruby and Opal. Oh, there you are Maude."

"Good to see you, Nadine. What are you up to today?" Ruby asked.

"Thank you so much for asking," Nadine smiled. "I've just come over from Junction. You might have heard that I was on the radio all morning."

"Were you now?" Ruby asked.

"Yes, yes. Such a lovely time. They interviewed me about that contest I won. You know the one I'm talking about Opal, and you, too, Maude. The one where the station partnered with Martin, my favorite travel agent," Nadine crooned.

"Martin's been my travel agent and friend for twenty years," Maude snapped.

Nadine ignored her and continued on. "Well, they finally had me on the air to announce the grand prize.

14

Y'all will never guess what I won!" Nadine cooed. "Or should I say earned."

"Sit on down a spell and do tell," Opal smiled. She and Ruby sat back down in their chairs.

The only open seat was next to Maude, who cut her eyes at Opal. Nadine, in a state of happiness, either didn't notice or care about Maude's grumpy scowl. She sank down in the empty seat and pulled her sunglasses down to the bridge of her nose.

"An all-expenses paid round trip!" Nadine squealed.

"Wow, that's amazing!" Ruby smiled.

"Where to?" Opal asked.

"For a whole week!" Nadine continued.

"Where to?" Opal asked again.

"Flight, hotel, and two hundred dollars cash for meals," Nadine exclaimed.

"Where are you going?" Opal asked.

"I can't wait. It's going to be amazing," Nadine sighed happily.

"Where are you going?" Opal implored.

"It's an early morning flight, of course," Nadine grinned. "But that's perfectly alright."

"Where in the hell are you going?" Maude bellowed.

"Only the grandest city in the entire world," Nadine smiled.

"I doubt that," Maude snickered.

"Paris?" Ruby guessed.

"Milan?" Opal offered.

"No, and no," beamed Nadine.

"WHERE?" bellowed Maude.

"The one and only New York City!" Nadine grinned.

∽ Chapter Two ∽

The drinking glass Maude had been holding shattered on the floor.

"I'm sorry, where did you say you were going?" Ruby asked, just in case she had misheard.

Nadine glared at Maude before turning back to Ruby. "New York City, as in the Big Apple," she smiled. "Surely you've heard it called that."

"No. Nope. Absolutely not," Maude interrupted. "No ma'am."

"Beg your pardon?" Nadine asked.

"Nope," Maude repeated. She shook her head and turned on her heels and walked towards the front door. Ruby and Opal turned towards the window and watched Maude open her car door and sit inside the driver's seat.

"What was all that about?" Nadine snapped.

"Well, it appears that Maude had somewhere else to be," Opal said diplomatically.

"Well, I just can't for the life of me understand what comes over that woman," Nadine shook her head. "Anyway, as I was saying, I'll be in New York City all next week."

"Next week?" squeaked Ruby.

"As in, the week after this current one?" Opal parroted.

"Yes," Nadine answered. "Are you ok, Ruby?"

Ruby's eyes had widened and she looked at Opal with a very strained look.

"Well, Nadine, this was lovely. Ruby, I'll pay the check up front, and well, this sure was nice, Nadine. I'll see you around," Opal smiled. She grabbed her purse in one hand and yanked Ruby towards the counter. "Go check on Maude while I settle this bill," Opal whispered.

Ruby nodded and walked outside to where Maude was still parked. She tapped on the window and Maude rolled it down slowly. Cigarette smoke billowed out of the open window.

"Maude! You're going to suffocate yourself like that!" Ruby shrieked.

"I'm trying to clear my mind," Maude huffed. She took a long drag from the cigarette and blew the smoke out slowly.

Opal appeared behind Ruby and shook her head. "Well, that was a great lunch," she smiled.

Even though Maude had her sunglasses on, Ruby knew she was cutting her eyes at Opal. She blew another cloud of smoke out of the window and put the cigarette out in the ashtray next to her.

"Have you cleared your head enough," coughed Opal.

"I think so," Maude nodded slowly. "We're leaving in a few days. Who knows when her trip is. By the time she goes, everyone will have already heard about our trip, so who cares."

"Well," Opal looked at Ruby sheepishly. "I don't know about all that."

"What do you mean?" Maude asked curtly.

"Just remember that New York is an awfully big city," Ruby gulped.

"Ruby?" Maude asked. They could hear the edge in her voice.

"And we probably won't even see her while we're there anyway," Ruby continued.

"We won't be seeing her because she won't be there," Maude stammered.

"Except she will be," Opal finished.

Maude's knuckles turned white as she gripped the steering wheel tightly.

"Just breathe through it, Maude. In through your nose, out through your mouth. In through your nose, out through your mouth," Opal instructed. "Are you holding your breath? See Ruby, I told you she holds her breath like a toddler when they're getting ready to throw a tantrum. She's fifty years old," Opal sighed.

"Maude, Opal's right. Relax and let it go. Don't let this little thing put a damper on our trip," Ruby said.

Maude swallowed hard and opened her mouth to say something, but must have thought better of it. She took a deep breath and released the steering wheel.

"Deep breaths," Opal repeated. "Yes! Just like that. Wait, where are you going?"

Maude had thrown the car into reverse and slowly backed out of the parking spot. She rolled up the window and without a backward glance, put the car in drive and left Ruby and Opal standing in the parking lot.

"Should we follow her?" Ruby asked.

"If Mavis threw a tantrum in the Piggly Wiggly, would you baby her?" Opal asked.

"Heavens no!" said Ruby.

"Exactly. She'll be fine. Though I wouldn't want to be Martin right now. I suspect he's about to get an earful on the phone when she gets home," Opal chuckled.

Ruby shook her head and fished the car keys out of her purse. "I've got to run by the grocery store and then pick up the kids. I've got to see Nadine tonight after that spectacle for Mavis' last voice lesson. Goodness, I cannot believe the scene she caused. And breaking that glass. I swear!"

"They were sweeping it up when I walked out. I left a big tip to cover it, don't worry about that. People around here are pretty used to Maude," Opal chuckled.

Ruby shook her head again and sighed. "Well, thank you for lunch. Hopefully, we'll be able to show our faces here again soon. I'll see you tomorrow evening, Opal."

Opal waved until Ruby was long gone out of the parking lot. She had a free afternoon ahead of her. It wasn't often that that happened. Being the owner of the premiere salon and spa in town was hectic, but Opal loved the thrill.

Speaking of thrill, it was high time that she felt that rush of the wind in her face. Staying bottled up in a hair salon all day every day wasn't good for her skin, so she made the spontaneous decision to drive over to Junction and rent a kayak. She was no stranger to the river. It was where she felt most at peace, surrounded by the weeds and wild animals. The crickets chirped, the bullfrogs croaked, and the turtles snapped at fish that swam by. Nature called out to her every time she paddled along the reeds.

Meanwhile, back in Rhinestone, Maude was on hold with Martin Rhodes, her travel agent, who also happened to be the sponsor for the radio contest that Nadine had won. The longer the music played, the sullener she became. After ten minutes of waiting, she slammed the phone back in the receiver, causing Buford, her new puppy, to fall off the couch where he had been enjoying an afternoon nap. "It's like being trapped in an elevator!"

Maude stood up from her chair and quickly stretched before turning to Buford.

"Come on Buford, let's go for a walk," Maude offered. She stuffed her pockets full of dog treats and grabbed a handful of cookies from the cookie jar to keep them both satisfied on their trek.

Buford scratched at the door and slowly made his way down the front steps. Maude followed him down the driveway to the stretch of grass by the mailbox. She would not let Nadine's presence ruin her trip. Opal and Ruby were right, not that she'd ever tell them that. New York City was large enough for all of them to have a good time. Nadine would have her own separate itinerary anyway.

Buford tuckered out after twenty minutes of being outside. He groaned loudly and refused to move another inch, so Maude had to reach down and pick the dramatic dog up. She lugged him the quarter mile back home and laid him on the couch before plopping down in her favorite recliner. She dozed off and on for the rest of the afternoon. Her snoring was interrupted by a sudden pounding on her front door. Maude lounged forward, caught her foot on the pop-up tray that had been strategically placed to hold all her snacks, and fell face first onto the floor. She stood up quickly to try to stop the glass of sweet tea from spilling completely, but it was too late.

"Who in the world is trying to beat my door down?" Maude fumed as she snatched the door open.

"Well it's about time! I thought I was going to have to climb through the window," Opal sang.

"Why are you trying to break into my house?" Maude demanded.

"Oh, I just wanted to see if you were busy," Opal said. She pushed Maude out of the way and waltzed in.

"Where've you been? You stink!" Maude held her nose.

"On the river," Opal smiled. "What have you been doing? Your hair has seen better days."

"I took a nap," Maude shrugged.

Opal nodded. "You always get so tired after those temper tantrums."

"I had to talk to Buford for a walk," Maude sighed.

"I still don't know why you have to call every dog you get Buford," Opal interrupted.

"It's tradition," Maude explained. "My parents always named their dogs Rusty, so I continued the tradition."

"Doesn't that get weird though? Every time one passes on, you get a new one with the same name?" Opal asked bewilderedly.

"It's simpler that way," Maude shrugged. "I just reuse the collar and dog tag."

"It amazes me that you can find every stray dog in the county that's knocking on death's door and keep them on life support for a couple of years," Opal continued. "There was Buford the bulldog, and before that you had two mutts and then a blood hound mix. All of them were named Buford and they were the most pitiful creatures God ever made. That overweight basset hound was pretty great though."

"He was the best dog there ever was," sighed Maude. "Really miss that old' hound."

"Is that what possessed you to get a puppy this time?" Opal asked.

"Yeah, this one is a little more hyper than I remember though," Maude nodded. "He was the last one in the truck bed over at the Piggly Wiggly. They were practically giving him away. He was too cute to leave behind, even if he is a little cross-eyed," Maude shrugged.

"Always the heart for the less fortunate," Opal chuckled.

Maude rolled her eyes and looked out the front window towards the road. "What time is it?"

Opal looked at her watch and back at the clock on Maude's wall. "Either half past four or eleven thirty," she shrugged.

"What?" Maude asked.

"Your clock says one thing and my watch says another. I don't think either is right though," Opal smiled.

Maude rolled her eyes again and walked to the kitchen to check the digital clock on the microwave on the counter. "You know the battery died in the wall clock."

"That was six months ago," Opal said.

"It's right at least twice a day," Maude shrugged.

"Well that's one more than you usually are," Opal said.

"It's nearly seven o'clock," Maude grumbled. "No wonder I'm hungry! Let's go eat something."

"Ok," Opal agreed. "I'm feeling a good salad after being outside all afternoon."

"You can have your rabbit food, but I'm getting a steak. Let's go to The Big Steer," Maude offered. She said goodbye to Buford and grabbed her purse by the door. "I'll drive."

"We'll get there in record time," Opal laughed.

"I'd ask Ruby and them to come, but they've already eaten by this time," Maude acknowledged.

"Ruby and Mavis are at Nadine's, remember?" Opal reminded her.

"Oh, that's right," frowned Maude. She locked the front door behind her and strained to see Nadine's house down the street. "Did you see that?"

"What?" Opal asked.

"I swear I saw something around those bushes," Maude said, still squinting into the distance.

"I don't see anything," Opal stood beside her.

Maude suddenly broke into a giant smile. "I guess it wouldn't hurt to stop in and check on things."

"What do you mean check in?" Opal asked. "I thought you were starving?"

"It'll only take a minute," Maude countered.

"Famous last words," Opal sighed. She climbed into the passenger seat of Maude's car and rolled down the window to help filter out the heavy cigarette smoke.

Maude backed the bright red Camaro out of her driveway and peeled into Nadine's driveway moments later. Before Opal could steady herself, Maude had already flown out of the car and zoomed up Nadine's front steps. She motioned for Opal to hurry up and get out of the car.

Opal took a few seconds to catch her breath and straightened up and walked towards Maude who was already banging on the front door.

"Calm down," Opal hissed. "You're going to scare the devil out of everyone inside."

"Like you did me a while ago?" Maude asked.

"That was different. I thought you might be dead. At your age you never really know," Opal shrugged.

Nadine flung open the door and in a huff. "What in the world are you doing here?"

Opal waved meekly behind Maude. She could see Ruby and Mavis peering around the corner.

"I thought I'd be the bigger person and come over here and warn you that there's a polecat sniffing around your azalea bushes," Maude said with a bit more of a smile than she intended.

"Really, Maude! You are the limit!" Nadine began.

"Suit yourself, but you have a skunk digging around the shrubs out there," Maude motioned to the side of the porch.

"Technically, a polecat is a weasel and not a skunk," Opal added quickly. "I thought everyone knew that," she mumbled.

"Well, this one was a skunk," Maude said.

"Of all crazy things you have come up with over the years, Maude, this takes the cake," Nadine fumed.

"Anyway, we're heading to dinner and saw Ruby's car in the drive. Just thought we'd save you from disaster, Ruby," Maude answered nonchalantly.

"Didn't you just see each other a few hours ago?" Nadine scowled. "When you so rudely stormed out of the diner."

Maude shifted uncomfortably on her feet. "Well, I had just remembered something that I needed to do," she began.

"Of course," Nadine smiled. "Anyway, as you can see, there's something that I need to be doing." She turned around and smiled genuinely at Mavis and Ruby. "Let's get back to your voice lesson, precious. Maude was just leaving."

Nadine forcibly closed the front door in Maude's face, leaving her looking aghast. Opal chuckled and added, "Nadine has a little moxie after all."

"That old cow!" stomped Maude. "Can you believe that!"

"Yes, I can. And good for her. Now come on, let's get on to dinner and get you fed before you burn down the town like Sherman marching to the sea," Opal laughed.

Maude crossed her arms and slunk down the porch back to her car that was still running. They made it to the steakhouse five minutes later.

"Who knew that red lights were optional," Opal mused sarcastically.

"I had plenty of time. They're suggestions at best," Maude said seriously.

"I don't think that's right, but the laws of traffic have always meant something different to you," Opal winked.

They walked inside the restaurant past the giant cow head on the wall. The host sat them at a booth in the center of the restaurant, which was something that Maude would have generally protested, but she was too hungry to care. They ordered their drinks and

Maude asked for two glasses of tea so that she wouldn't have to ask for a refill.

"You sure are in a mood tonight," Opal mumbled.

Maude ignored her and looked over the menu. "I want the biggest steak they have. And a double helping of fries."

"I don't know where you store it. If I ate like you did, I'd be my own continent," Opal pondered aloud.

"Good genes," Maude mumbled.

"I've seen you in jeans, and I beg to differ," Opal smiled.

Before Maude could retort, the waiter handed them their drinks and quickly took down their orders. He returned moments later with a basket of rolls and a double helping of butter.

"I still can't believe she slammed the door in my face," Maude said.

"Are you back on that?" Opal sighed. "You practically blew her door down like the big bad wolf!"

"I ain't done it," Maude said. "I was just trying to be neighborly and warn her about the skunk."

"You're a nosey old broad," Opal mumbled. "You know good and well you didn't see a skunk."

"Not nosey, just involved," Maude corrected. "And I did, too!"

"Overly involved," Opal replied.

"Well if that ain't the pot calling the kettle black!" Maude huffed. "You know every secret in Rhinestone before it's even told!"

"And I keep every one of them," Opal said. "I can't help it if I'm so trustworthy."

"You could write a book someday," Maude admitted. "One of those juicy ones. I'd read it. Well, as long as I'm not mentioned."

"I don't have the time nor the energy to write a book," Opal said. "And you don't read."

"I might if it was good," Maude shrugged.

The waiter interrupted their banter and set their entrees down in front of them. Opal's tossed salad was as colorful as a Christmas tree. Maude's steak took up half the platter. The double order of fries barely fit on the other half. No one had ever been able to finish the forty-eight-ounce steak before, but Maude set her mind to finish it.

It didn't take her long either. Opal had barely finished her salad and second glass of iced tea when Maude pushed herself away from the table and savored the last bite of beef. She patted her stomach and drained her fourth glass of tea before sighing heavily.

"Guess I'll drive us home," Opal said. "You're going to feel that tomorrow. All that red meat is going to make you bloat."

"It was worth it," Maude sighed happily.

~Chapter Three~

The old school gymnasium was warm with so many people crammed inside that Friday evening. The folding chairs were close together and people scrambled for seats to see their children perform. Ruby had, of course, gotten there early to reserve seats for her group on the front row.

Mavis looked adorable in her periwinkle blue dress and pigtails with ribbons tied at the ends. She had been very nervous for her upcoming performance, but Jameson had promised her a trip to the ice cream shop after supper. Mavis loved ice cream sundaes best of all, so there was a new pep in her step when Ruby hugged her goodbye behind the stage.

Round Trip

Ruby hurried to her seat in between Jameson and Wilbur as soon as Mavis was settled. Maude and Opal squeezed in next to them with a small bouquet of flowers and a plastic bag full of peanut butter cookies.

"Aw, Mavis will love the flowers and cookies!" Ruby smiled.

"Oh? I brought the cookies for my snack, but yes, the flowers are mighty pretty," Maude replied.

Jameson chuckled and reached for a cookie for himself. "These are good! Did you make them?"

"You know Maude doesn't bake," Opal laughed. "We picked them up from the bakery next to the salon."

Principal Harvey walked onto the makeshift stage and stood behind the podium. "Welcome everyone to our annual talent showcase. Boy do we have some talent in this school this year! In between acts, make sure you walk to the back of the gym and bid on a cake or two. Our dessert sale always brings in some good revenue for the school. This year's proceeds will be going towards a new floor for the gym. Once we rip this one up, we'll be selling pieces of the old floor for nostalgia, so make sure you stay up to date on the progress. Anyway, let's give a round of applause for our hostess this evening, Ms. Nadine Waters!"

Magnolia Manor

A smattering of applause resounded in the gym. Nadine pranced across the stage and curtsied in front of Principal Harvey. She wore a small tiara and a bright pink gown that trailed after her. Maude couldn't help but roll her eyes at the sight. Nadine never let anyone forget that she was the very first Miss Rhinestone nearly thirty-five years ago. All of the girls in their school had been forced to do the pageant, which turned out to be a successful fundraiser for the new gymnasium the school desperately needed. Opal had been named Miss Congeniality and was the first runner up to Nadine, who gloated for weeks. She rarely missed an opportunity for the rest of the school year to tease Maude about placing last behind Betsy Warner, a girl whose eyes pointed in every direction but straight. Maude, for her part, hadn't cared about the pageant, as was evident by the coveralls she paraded across the stage in instead of an evening gown. Losing to Betsy was a bit of a shock, but considering Betsy had bloomed early, as they say, perhaps it was not too surprising that the student body consisting mainly of teenage boys cast more of their votes her way for the People's Choice Award.

Round Trip

Decades later, Nadine still managed to find excuses to wear her tiara and sash to events. As the reigning hospitality chairwoman for the Ladies Auxiliary Club, it was her sworn duty to the community of Rhinestone to ensure that every new business had the best grand opening event possible, including the deer processing plant, the Big Rack, and the laundromat, The Sudsy Mart. There was great concern that her tiara wouldn't survive the car wash grand opening a few weeks ago. Maude was not-so-secretly hoping that both the crown and Nadine would get a thorough soaking at Sammy's Spit Shine, but much to Maude's chagrin, Nadine survived unscathed.

"Welcome everyone! Let's give a round of applause for Principal Harvey and the ladies of the PTO who have worked so hard to bring us all this special evening," Nadine beamed.

"She's acting like this is a durn pageant," Maude grumbled.

"As many of you may know, the school has decided to bring back the Miss Rhinestone pageant this fall. It will not only help the school raise money for new projects, but inspire generations of young ladies. I know I am a far better person for being crowned the inaugural Miss Rhinestone. I remember it like it was yesterday. It was certainly life-changing for those of us who took it seriously," she cut her eyes at Maude on the front row.

"Shh, don't respond," Opal warned. She elbowed Maude hard in the gut, causing her to spit out pieces of her peanut butter cookie.

"The pageant will be a wonderful way to celebrate the centennial of our beautiful town. Rhinestone officially turns one hundred years old this spring! Yes, another round of applause!" Nadine exclaimed. Once the crowd quieted back down, she continued. "At the end of this month, the Ladies Auxiliary will be burying our very own time capsule. We are looking for items that represent the history of our beautiful city, as well as the present, so please be thinking of items to seal inside. All inquiries and submissions can be presented at the next Auxiliary meeting at the Chamber of Commerce. Thank you Mayor Humperdink for partnering with the Ladies Auxiliary. It's so wonderful to see everyone coming together for this historical celebration. And now, without further ado, let's give a round of applause for little miss Mary Donahue who will be performing a tap dance routine to a song written by her father, who will be picking the banjo for us! What a treat!"

After Mary and her father were finished, Sammy and Stephen Hatcher performed a puppet show. Then, Mona, the daughter of the café owners, whispered a song about her mother's famous apple pie, followed by Donovan Marks who sang "This Little Light of Mine." The Perkins twins hula-hoop routine sent a hula-hoop flying out into the audience, but no one was injured. Maude had already nodded off to sleep and missed the chaos. She woke suddenly to Opal elbowing her again.

"Wake up, Mavis is next!" Opal whispered.

Maude shifted in her seat and sat up straight. "What is she singing?" she leaned over and asked Ruby.

"I'm not sure exactly," Ruby admitted. "She's been working with Nadine, and they say it's a surprise. During her voice lessons, I usually read a book or do my grocery shopping."

Mavis walked shyly towards the center of the stage and looked down at her feet. Jameson waved and smiled, which gave her a burst of confidence. Mavis took a deep breath and belted out a high note that made them all jump. No accompaniment music was needed. It did not take them long to figure out what song Mavis had been working on.

"Oh my," gasped Ruby.

"Well, this sure is something," Jameson coughed.

"I don't think this about baking," Wilbur whispered.

Jameson coughed into his handkerchief again to muffle his laughter. "I think you may be right, son."

"Well, it's pretty entertaining, whatever it is," Wilbur chuckled. He looked behind Ruby who was doubled over in shame to catch Opal's eye. She winked at him and covered her mouth with her hand to keep herself from laughing out loud.

"Thank you, Mavis. That was a great version of "Pour Some Sugar on Me." Next we have Billy Akins showing off his impressive deer antler collection. Not sure how that's exactly a talent, but nonetheless," Nadine smiled. She ushered Mavis offstage and disappeared behind the curtain.

Ruby didn't lift her head out of her lap until the award for most talented went to the Perkins twins. Jameson fetched Mavis while Ruby, Wilbur, Maude, and Opal gathered their things.

"Great job, sugar. That was, well, entertaining," Jameson smiled at Mavis who was eagerly awaiting his praise. He turned his attention to Nadine who was standing nearby. "And Nadine, what can I say? Thank you for working so hard with Mavis this past month."

"We had been working on a nice little Whitney Houston medley, but Mavis said she wanted to try something different last night after Maude practically busted in on our rehearsal. She said it was to honor Maude. I reckon it's Maude's favorite song or something. Mavis is such a little angel," Nadine beamed. "Those high notes just come so natural to her."

Jameson wasn't sure that Def Leppard's newest hit was the best choice of song for an eight-year-old girl to sing, but Nadine was right, Mavis did have a great voice for that genre. He steered Mavis through the crowd to where Ruby, Wilbur, Maude, and Opal were still sitting.

"Big Mama! Did you love my song?" Mavis asked.

Ruby nodded and hugged Mavis tightly. "It was definitely a surprise," she agreed.

"Where'd you hear that song?" Opal asked Mavis.

"In Ms. Maude's car. I told Ms. Nadine it was her favorite song because she played it all the time," Mavis smiled.

Ruby snapped her attention to Maude and raised her eyebrows.

"I, I don't know what you're talking about," Maude gulped.

"Yes ma'am, when you picked me and Wilbur up from school last month when Big Mama was at the hospital with Grandmother Montgomery, it played in your car two times. I knew you must love it," Mavis smiled. "And then you sang it at the kitchen last Sunday at supper time."

"I can't help what comes on the radio," Maude hissed to Ruby.

"I remember that," Wilbur nodded. "You and Ms. Opal were talking about your new puppy you had just got and it came on the different radio stations. I didn't know those were the exact words, but it has a catchy beat."

Jameson roared in laughter and slapped his knee. "Well I'll be!" he laughed. "How about we head over to Paula's Pizza and end this night with some breadsticks and pizza?"

"And ice cream," Mavis reminded him. "I did so good, I can have two sundaes, right Big Daddy?"

"Right you are!" Jameson agreed.

Paula's Pizza had a pizza and pasta buffet that children and adults both fawned over. It also happened to be next door to the ice cream shop that Mavis loved. After eating the fill of pizza and ice cream, Jameson drove Ruby, Mavis, and Wilbur back home to the Manor. Opal and Maude promised they'd be over sometime tomorrow afternoon to go over their trip information one last time.

When Jameson and Ruby put Mavis to bed that night, she offered to do another performance for them. They politely declined and tucked her into bed. Later that evening in their recliners, Jameson was still chuckling.

"You won't find finer entertainment like that old talent show in New York City," he laughed. "But I sure am glad y'all are finally getting to go on your big trip. Then again, the three of you always seem to find adventure wherever you go."

"We sure do," Ruby agreed. "I wrote down the hotel name and phone number and all of our flight information by the telephone. Don't forget."

"Everything is going to be fine," Jameson smiled. "I know you get nervous every time you travel."

"It's just such a long trip," Ruby smiled fretfully.

"And you're going to love every minute of it!" Jameson added. "Even if you end up in Nepal or Albania again."

"No more international travel for me," laughed Ruby.

"You know, you can't make up half the adventures you three get into," Jameson laughed. "Let's try to stay out of jail this go 'round, too," he winked. "Though if y'all do get in trouble, I'll hop on the first flight out there. Mavis and Wilbur would love a good look at the big city," he laughed.

Ruby shook her head and caught his smile. "I still can't believe we're flying into New York and get to explore the city. This has been our dream of ours for so long," she said. "Thank you for taking care of everything here."

"Of course," Jameson nodded. "The three of us are planning on getting into all sorts of trouble while y'all are gone."

Ruby shook her head again and laughed. "Now that would be something new."

Maude and Opal arrived the next afternoon with smiles plastered across their faces. They were visibly bubbly about their upcoming trip.

"We'll be ready at eight tomorrow morning," Maude reminded Ruby. "Probably before. So if you want to leave the Manor before seven, we can be ready. I can be ready in fifteen minutes if need be."

"We've already agreed on leaving your house at eight tomorrow morning," Ruby smiled. "Opal and I have already reminded you that we have a Ladies Auxiliary meeting this evening, remember?"

"I know," Maude grumbled. "And I already said I wasn't going. I've got to take Buford over to my great-nephew's house and get him settled in. I still can't believe y'all roped me into joining that snooze fest."

Ruby and Opal had been members of the Ladies Auxiliary for years. Finally, right before their annual Christmas banquet, they managed to get Maude to join.

"Maude's so excited, she's liable to start walking if you're a minute late. Ruby," Opal laughed.

"Ruby won't be late," Maude corrected. "Of course, I could always drive if that works better."

"No," said Ruby, Opal, and Jameson at the same time.

Mavis giggled from across the room. She was hovering over her coloring book eating a bowl of banana pudding.

"I'm an excellent driver," Maude shrugged.

"And apparently you play great music, too," Opal said slyly under her breath.

Maude's ears turned a light shade of pink. She shushed Opal and hurriedly changed the subject. "What do you all have planned while we're gone?" she asked Jameson.

"Wilbur and I have a date with the river for some fishing, for sure. Mavis has decided that we're going to the movie theatre a few evenings," Jameson chuckled. "I also plan on visiting with Mother quite a bit, too. Ever since she fell and broke her hip last month, she hasn't been the same," he lamented.

"I was hoping she was doing better," Opal grimaced. "I'll send some of those herbal tea leaves she likes. You've got a key to my house, so on your way over to the nursing home, stop by and I'll leave the packages on the counter."

"Thank you," Jameson smiled. "She'll like that."

The front door opened and Wilbur walked in and smiled.

"Wilbur? There he is!" smiled Maude. "Where have you been?"

"I took a walk in the woods," he smiled. "It's so quiet and peaceful out there."

Opal nodded. "Nothing like it," she agreed. "See anything interesting?"

Wilbur took off his jacket and hung it up by the door. He walked into the kitchen and opened his bag up for them to see. "I found these out in the woods. What do you think they are?" He held up three beautiful gemstones that shone in the light.

Opal gasped and held her hand to her mouth. Wilbur's grin was unmistakable. Neither Jameson, Ruby, Maude, or Mavis could understand what was going on.

"Well I'll be," exclaimed Opal. She returned Wilbur's smile and shook her head thoughtfully. "I've never seen them out there before."

"What are they?" Maude asked. She touched one of the stones and looked puzzled.

"They're opals," Wilbur grinned.

"Opal's? You mean this clown dropped them?" Maude asked.

Wilbur and Opal both giggled. "They're real-life opals, gemstones," Wilbur smiled. "I've never seen one in real life, but I knew what they looked like from one of my textbooks. I kept digging, but I could only find these three."

"They're beautiful," exclaimed Ruby.

"Oh!" breathed Maude. "I bet they're worth a pretty penny."

"They are," nodded Opal. "Great job finding these, Wilbur. They're mighty rare and indeed precious."

"Good for you, son!" said Jameson. "We can run you over to Bill's over at the jewelry store in Junction one day next week if you'd like."

Wilbur shook his head. "No sir." He turned to Ruby, Opal, and Maude and smiled. "I want you three to have them."

"No!" gasped Opal, Maude, and Ruby together, but Wilbur merely smiled.

"There's three of them, on the Manor's property, and named after one the Stone Sisters. It's fate," he grinned.

"Oh Wilbur," Ruby wiped a tear from her eye.

"You can each have one. Definitely fate," Wilbur nodded. He washed his hands in the kitchen sink and allowed each of the three women to squeeze him in a hug.

✐ Chapter Four ✐

The Ladies Auxiliary met at Beaver Crossing Holy Church for the Faithful. It was a time of great fellowship, gossip, and hard work. The ladies on the board were in charge of many wonderful ideas in the city of Rhinestone. Their cookbook fundraiser a few years ago singlehandedly funded the fellowship hall. Rhinestone Recipes was still a hot ticket item that was printed in bulk every few months. Bakers as far as Arkansas and North Carolina had inquired about the treasured collection of recipes passed down throughout the families and history of Rhinestone.

To kick off the meeting, the women sat down for a potluck supper together. There was an agreed upon theme for every meeting, and each woman signed up to bring something related to that theme. After a potluck supper of finger foods, the women sat down around one of the long rectangular tables in the fellowship hall and got down to business. They were in charge of the Rhinestone Centennial Celebration next month, and there wasn't anyone more excited than Nadine, who was in charge of the time capsule. She passed around a sign-up sheet for people to write down ideas for the time capsule. Sue offered to donate one of the bricks from the chimney in her home, which was the oldest standing home in Rhinestone. Leanne offered to include an arrowhead from her family's private collection. There were photographs and maps and a copy of Rhinestone Recipes to be included. As soon as the latest copy of the Rhinestone Register was printed, it too would be placed in the giant stainless-steel box.

After the sheet was passed around, Nadine sent around a mockup of a poster detailing the date and time for the town picnic. Food was the centerpiece for all Rhinestone functions, as southern hospitality was always the driving force behind these kinds of events. The town square in the center of downtown was the perfect meeting place for the town picnic, as it had the most beautiful, empty field under a group of tall oak trees. Families were encouraged to bring their own blankets, chairs, and picnic tables to spread out across the field.

Nadine suddenly interrupted their chatter. "I just need to take a minute and tell y'all about what happened to me today. This morning I woke up to a big, gorgeous sign in my front yard telling me I had won best yard for the county. I didn't even know I was a finalist," Nadine gushed. "You know the county does this twice a year, and to be a winner, well, it just feels so right."

"Probably all that fertilizer," Opal whispered underneath her breath to Ruby.

Ruby smiled and shook her head slightly. "Maybe Maude will finally learn to let things be."

"Doubtful," chuckled Opal.

"Well, this wraps up tonight's meeting," Nadine smiled. "I'll be out of town for the next little while. So will Opal and Ruby. Next meeting will be at the Chamber offices as a joint meeting with the Mayor and city council. Principal Harvey and the PTO ladies will also be joining us. We will nail down the time capsule items, pass out the flyers and posters for the picnic, and turn in all sponsorship money. Y'all remember to spread the word about the different events. This is going to be major news, I just know it!"

The women gathered up their folders and purses and turned out the lights to the building. Ellen locked the door behind them, and they all said goodnight on the way to their respective cars.

"Well, I'll see you bright and early," Opal grinned.

"See you then," Ruby replied. She smiled the entire way back to the Manor.

True to her word, Ruby was on the road before eight o'clock the next morning. She hugged Wilbur and Mavis goodbye at the breakfast table and followed Jameson out the door to her Buick. He loaded her luggage in the trunk and held the door open for her.

"Y'all have the best time," he smiled. "Just try and stay out of trouble," he winked.

"I can't make any promises," Ruby smiled back. "I'll call you once we get checked into the hotel."

The sun was shining brightly through a light blanket of clouds as Ruby pulled into Opal's driveway. As she climbed up the front porch steps, she could already hear the commotion inside.

"Maude, will you calm down. Goodness, you're wearing a hole in the carpet with all your pacing," Opal told her.

"I can't help it. I'm ready to go. I thought she'd be here by now," Maude looked at her watch again.

"I'm sure she's on her way. We did say to meet here at eight o'clock," Opal said. "It's five til."

"There she is!" Maude shouted from the window. She threw open the front door to see Ruby standing on the neon purple doormat. "It's about time."

"Thank goodness. Maude's been worrying me to death," Opal mumbled. She took another sip of her lukewarm coffee that Maude had brought over and grimaced. Maude wasn't the best when it came to making coffee. She never measured the right amount of grounds or made sure the water was hot enough. Opal poured the remainder of the brown liquid down her sink and rinsed the cup thoroughly.

"Good morning, Maude. Y'all ready to go?" Ruby called good naturedly.

"She's been ready since before seven o'clock. She spent the last hour walking the floor like a madwoman," Opal told Ruby.

"I'm not mad. I'm in a great mood," Maude looked at them.

"Mad as in crazy," Opal explained. She picked up her two suitcases and slung her backpack over her shoulder.

"Now aint that the pot calling the kettle black," Maude replied as she too picked up her suitcase and purse. "Let's get these loaded in Ruby's trunk. We ain't got all day."

Ruby held the door open for them and followed them down the steps to the waiting car. "She's like a kid in a candy shop," Ruby laughed to Opal.

"You have no idea," Opal shook her head. "She barely let me eat my breakfast in peace."

"I wouldn't call that brown paste breakfast," added Maude.

"It's my own mixture of oatmeal and hazelnuts," Opal said. "I offered you some."

"And I near about gagged when you did. No thanks. I had my bacon and eggs before I got to your house," Maude said.

"Are we good to head straight to the airport?" Ruby asked Maude.

Maude wheeled around on her heel. "That's the plan! Where else would we go?"

"I'm just making sure," Ruby assured her. "How did Buford like it when you took him to your nephew's house last night?"

"He's having the time of his life. A house full of kids and all that farmland. He may never want to come home," Maude laughed. She wedged the final bag into the trunk and slammed it shut. "Are we ready?"

"We're waiting on you!" Opal said. "You're losing that pep in your step a little more every day."

"Don't start with me, Opal Tyler!" Maude glared.

"Well, sometimes the truth hurts," Opal hummed as she got into the passenger seat.

Maude mumbled something under her breath while dutifully climbing into the backseat with their carry-on bags. Before she could get comfortable, Ruby started the car and began backing out of Opal's driveway.

"Oh wait!" Opal shouted.

'What is it?" Maude demanded.

"I think I left my humidifier plugged in," Opal said. She opened the door and jumped out before either Ruby or Maude could say anything. Five minutes later, she was back in the passenger seat.

"Are we good now?" Maude asked.

"Of course we are," Opal replied before suddenly getting a far-off look in her eyes. "Oh, wait a minute." Before she could finish her thought, she was gone again.

"What now?" Maude asked while she and Ruby watched Opal scamper up the porch steps again.

"Who knows?" Ruby shrugged.

Maude looked at her watch and gritted her teeth. "I swear if she makes us late, I'm shoving her in my suitcase."

Opal sashayed back to the car a few minutes later and sat back down in the passenger seat. "Sorry, I had to make sure I didn't leave the kettle on the stove," Opal hummed.

"You have got to be kidding me!" Maude fumed in the backseat.

"So we're all good? We're ready to go now?" Ruby asked.

"Yep!" Opal said. She stared at Ruby for a second and blinked heavily. "Wait a minute! How could I forget!"

"I'm going to kill her!" Maude said as they watched Opal trek up the porch steps for the third time.

They watched Opal turn the front door handle and make sure the door was officially locked. She casually walked back to the car where her friends were still waiting to leave.

"Always best to check twice. Sometimes three times. You can never be too careful," Opal said solemnly.

"I've seen you leave your front door wide open more times than I can count," Maude snapped.

"Let it go," whispered Ruby. "Ok, now we're ready." Ruby put the car in reverse again and began to back out of the driveway.

"Oops! One more thing!" Opal sang.

"Opal Clementine Tyler, if you leave this car again, I will personally hog tie you to the top of this vehicle," Maude snapped.

"I have to say goodbye to my chickens," Opal said. She moved to open the door, but Maude was quicker. She held Opal around the neck and squeezed her arm. "Fine," groaned Opal. "I'll yell from the window. Goodbye Leroy, Little Maude, Rue, Petunia, Frankie, Clara, Belle, Jasmine, Naydina, Winnie, Lulu, Ellis, and Pepper!" Opal called out the window. "You're such good little hens," she coughed.

"Ruby, if you don't back out of this God forsaken driveway faster, I'm tying you up, too," Maude said sternly.

Ruby rolled her eyes, but backed out quicker than usual. "Who's going to look after your chickens?" wondered Ruby as they pulled onto the highway. "I can ask Jameson if he'll look in on them."

"Mortie's got it covered," Opal smiled. "He has such a way with them."

"Dead people and chickens. What a combination!" Maude whistled.

Ruby glared at her from the rearview mirror. "That's very sweet of him," she smiled at Opal.

"Oh, he's such a sweetheart. He really has a way with people. He's such a busy man these days, what with his crematorium opening in Junction and the funeral parlor here in Rhinestone. He's finally a chain, which is what he always wanted. But he always makes time for me," Opal beamed.

"On top of being the county coroner, too," added Ruby. "Sounds like he needs a vacation."

"Oh, he can't take a vacation, Ruby," Opal said quickly. "He has to deal with the worst of the worst on a daily basis. Car accidents, disease, and well, you know death never sleeps."

"Can we please change the subject?" Maude asked. She was looking a little green in the backseat.

"All that sewage coffee finally catching up to you?" Opal asked.

"No," shouted Maude. "I'm just ready to be there is all. Ruby doesn't make good time like I do."

"Thank goodness," Opal said. "The last time you drove to the airport you almost killed us all!"

"The last time she drove us anywhere is always a struggle," laughed Ruby.

"I'm a great driver. I keep telling y'all that," Maude said. "No accidents have gone down on my record."

"That's a miracle in itself," Opal said.

"Hush up!" Maude told her. "How much longer do we have till we're there?"

"We just got on the road," Opal told her.

"Yeah, but I can't wait to get there. I thought we'd be closer by now," Maude told them.

"Why don't you take a nap?" Ruby suggested. "That always helps Mavis on car rides."

"Need me to sing you a lullaby?" Opal volunteered.

"I think I'm good," Maude said, but Opal launched into a ballad about a man travelling through time with his pet hippopotamus.

"Okay, okay! I'll stop asking about the time, but for the love of all that is holy, stop singing about the hippopotamus," Maude covered her ears.

"You don't like my new material?" Opal asked.

"It's not a classic," Maude admitted.

"That's because you don't know true musical talent," Opal shrugged. "You're too busy listening to Def Leppard."

"They came on the radio station I was listening to. It's not like I went out and bought the album or anything," Maude said.

"Honestly, I'm kind of impressed that you even know the song. You're not cool like I am," Opal nodded. Maude merely rolled her eyes.

By the time they pulled into the parking deck of the airport, Maude was ready to fly solo. "I couldn't take one more minute of that car ride," she mumbled.

"It was an easy drive and we have plenty of time to spare," Ruby shrugged.

"If you say so," Maude said. She handed Ruby and Opal their bags and led the way to their terminal.

When they got to their assigned gate, they had thirty minutes before they could board. Before Ruby could even think about visiting the nearest gift shop, Maude shut that down. "Save room for the shopping in New York. Let's find a bathroom and make sure we're ready for the flight," Maude instructed. "I want to be the first ones on the plane and the first ones off."

Opal shrugged and followed behind Maude who led the way to the nearest bathrooms. The airport was bustling with people. The three women had a hard time finding seats at the gate when they returned from the restrooms.

"Looks like a full flight," Opal said.

"No funny business this time," Maude said warily. "I mean it."

"Cross my heart," Opal swore. "I know you don't like to fly. I promise that Ruby and I will be on our best behavior."

Maude chewed the end of her fingernails and looked around. It was supposed to be a short flight into Washington D.C. where they would make a quick stop before flying the last little bit to New York City. Flying had never been her favorite thing. She preferred to keep her feet solidly on the ground.

Round Trip

They managed to find seats near each other. Opal plopped down next to a woman and her toddler, while Ruby took the window seat on the other side of the aisle. Maude stood on her tiptoes to see if there was an empty seat nearby, but the closest one was wedged between a priest and a nun.

"Swap with me Opal, please," Maude begged quietly.

Opal stood up in her seat to see where Maude was pointing. "No way," smiled Opal. "I've already made friends with little Wade here."

"You know nuns freak me out," Maude whispered.

"Hey sister!" Opal called to the nun three rows back. "My friend Maude wants to hear all about your history and the process of becoming a nun. She's very interested!"

"Opal, stop!" seethed Maude, but Opal merely smiled and turned her attention back to the adorable, chubby toddler and his mother.

Maude begrudgingly walked towards the empty seat and sank down. She was careful to not make eye contact with either the priest or the nun as she stowed her bag beneath her seat.

"One of these days," Maude mumbled. "I swear to God."

"I've never heard that prayer before, but don't let me stop you," the young priest smiled.

"Nice weather," the young nun smiled at Maude, who merely nodded. "Is this your first flight?"

Maude shook her head.

"It's my first flight," the nun smiled. "We are all going to Washington D.C. for a few days. What about you?"

"Lovely," squeaked Maude. She was trying to keep the coffee and breakfast from making a reappearance on the floor.

"Have you ever been to Washington? I'm sure we'll have a splendid time. There's a choir we'll be joining up with as part of a national prayer association," she prattled on.

"Isn't there a vow of silence you people take?" Maude gulped.

"A vow of silence?" she asked. "Oh no, I took a vow to sing!"

"Heaven help me," mumbled Maude.

"It surely can," the priest nodded.

"This is it, I'm in hell," mumbled Maude again.

Round Trip

The plane suddenly lurched forward, and Maude, ignoring the flight attendant's commands, hurdled the priest and ran down the center aisle towards the bathroom.

When she finally returned to her seat fifteen minutes later, the flight attendant handed her a stack of paper bags labeled for air sickness. Neither the priest or nun bothered to interrupt or comment on her intermittent moans. As soon as the plane's wheels finally touched the pavement, Maude let out a low sigh of relief.

"Thank God," Maude whimpered.

"Good day," the priest smiled at Maude. He patted her on the shoulder and grabbed his satchel and his Bible. Maude wasn't going anywhere, so he gingerly stepped over her and followed the flow of passengers off the plain.

The two-hour flight had been mostly peaceful turbulence wise, but that had not stopped Maude from gripping the armrests the entire time and leaning into her air sickness bag just in case. Flying would never be her preferred manner of travelling, no matter how many times she had flown.

Maude waited for a handful of nuns and other passengers to pass by before she snatched up her own bag and marched to the front of the plane. She glared at Opal who was waving to her from her seat.

"I swear to God," Maude began.

"You shouldn't swear!" Ruby hissed from her left. "I was hoping your seatmates would have changed you for the better."

"It wasn't that long of a flight," Opal laughed.

Maude ignored them both and scurried off the plane in a trot. Opal and Ruby hurried behind Maude as she exited the plane and headed towards a few empty chairs at the gate to wait out their one-hour layover.

"Those things are going to kill you," Opal told Maude as she reached in her purse and pulled out her cigarette case.

"Only if the plane crash doesn't," Maude mumbled.

"We're not going to crash, Maude," Ruby told her.

"I'm not going to waste the chance to have one last smoke in case we do," Maude said. She lifted the white cylinder to her mouth and lit it. After inhaling deeply, she sighed.

Ruby shook her head, but said nothing more. They all knew that Maude hated flying ever since their adventure almost thirty years earlier that had taken them halfway around the world. Maude had fared worse for the wear on that expedition, and she vowed to never get on a plane again. However, her need for a vacation every few months got in the way of that promise. If the destination was in driving distance, Maude preferred to drive. It was a testament to how badly she wanted to visit New York City that Maude had agreed to fly rather than spend two days driving.

"I'm going to check and see how long before we board the plane again," Opal said. She sprang up from her seat and skipped up to the gate counter.

"I'm picking the seats this time," Maude said to Ruby.

"Suit yourself," Ruby shrugged.

"We can board in thirty minutes," Opal smiled.

"Why couldn't we just stay on board?" Maude asked.

"Because it's a different plane. He said something about a smaller plane being brought in, but I zoned out," Opal shrugged.

"A smaller plane?" Maude fretted. "Why do we need a smaller plane?"

"Probably because New York is only a skip away," Opal smiled. "They don't need a big jet to take us down the street."

"Down the street?" Maude sniffed. "Why can't we just walk?"

"Well, I didn't literally mean down the street," Opal sighed. "She's so literal sometimes," Opal whispered to Ruby. "Metaphors escape her."

Maude took another long drag from her cigarette and cut her eyes at Opal. "How far are we?"

"About an hour," Opal pondered. "Give or take a few gusts of wind."

"Isn't there a car we rent?" Maude asked.

"There's a train," Opal offered.

"That's not much better," Maude said sourly.

"While you two argue about how we're getting to New York, I'm going to the restroom and then to see what kind of trinkets that shop over there has," Ruby interrupted.

"No one's arguing," Maude grumbled. "I just don't see why we couldn't have flown straight there. I told Martin to get the best deal and this is what he came up with," she mumbled to herself.

"I'm going with Ruby. Are you going to stay here being grumpy or come with us?" Opal asked.

"I'll stay here," Maude sighed.

"Ok," Opal shrugged. "Ruby, wait for me!" Opal called after Ruby, who had already walked off towards the restrooms.

The line for the restroom wasn't long, which gave Ruby and Opal more time in the gift shops that sold t-shirts, maps, books, hats, snacks, and souvenirs.

"I don't see anything I just have to have," Opal mused. "Oh, but I see that you do," giggled Opal. Ruby had shirts draped over her arm, a hat on her head, and a bag full of snacks.

"Maude loves these," Ruby said, gesturing to the rack of chips. "She's calmer when she's eating."

"Good idea," nodded Opal. "I'm going to walk down a ways and see what else is up here. I wish we had some real time to spend in Washington D.C., but that will be a trip for another time!"

"Keep an eye on your watch," Ruby reminded her.

Opal gave her a puzzled look and walked out of the store humming to herself. Opal's watch hadn't worked in years.

❧ Chapter Five ❧

"Where is she?" Maude demanded. She looked at her watch and back at the line of people who were boarding the airplane.

Ruby had come back to the seating area with a shopping bag full of apparel and a small bag full of snacks, but Opal was not with her.

"I was hoping she was back here with you," Ruby explained. She handed Maude the bag of snacks as a peace offering.

"I haven't seen her since she left with you," Maude retorted. "Wasn't she with you this whole time?"

"She was for a bit," Ruby said. "Then she left."

"Where'd she go?" gasped Maude.

"I don't know," Ruby sighed. Boarding had already begun and Opal was nowhere to be seen. "She said she was going to walk down a bit and see what other shops or restaurants they had. I told her to stay mindful of the time."

"Opal doesn't know time!" Maude screeched.

"She knows how to tell time," Ruby rolled her eyes. "Her watch is more expensive than mine is!"

"Ruby! That watch hasn't worked since God knows when! Aunt Willie gave her that years ago and I don't even know that it worked then," Maude hollered.

"Oh dear," Ruby winced. "Should we maybe tell someone?"

"Who are we going to tell?" Maude asked. "I swear, we need to put some kind of tracker on that woman! If they ever invent some sort of location tracker, she's getting one implanted right in her forehead!"

"Maybe they can make an announcement!" Ruby mused. She hurried over to the counter.

"Opal isn't going to listen to any kind of announcement! She's in her own little world," Maude mumbled, but Ruby was already pouring out the story to the man behind the counter.

Maude searched under every seat in the rows, but there was no sign of Opal.

"Are you looking for something?" one of the airline employees asked.

"Yes, her name is Opal," Maude said. "She wandered off and I can't find her."

"Oh no! Is she missing? Do you think someone may have taken her or maybe she followed someone by mistake?" the woman asked.

"She's missing all right. And this ain't the first time either," Maude nodded.

"Oh ma'am, this has happened before? You must be a nervous wreck! Are you two travelling alone? Travelling at your age with a small child is hard. Do you need me to get a stroller for her? I can print you a pass so that you can board first with her on any future flights. We always let women with babies and small children board first," she explained.

"Huh? What are you talking about? A child? What does my age have to do with a hill of beans?" Maude asked.

"You're missing a child, right? Your granddaughter, I assume? Or is it your great-granddaughter?" the woman asked.

"What? She ain't my granddaughter. I'm too young for grandchildren! Great-grandchild? I have you know I'm younger than I look! And Opal ain't a child. Well, not in that sense," Maude snapped.

"You're not looking for a child?" the woman asked. "I'm sorry, I'm so confused right now. What?"

"No!" Maude answered. "My friend has wandered off again. She does this all the time!"

"Just to clarify, you aren't missing a child?" the airline worker asked again.

"No! How many times do I have to tell you? Opal's a grown woman! Supposedly!" Maude snapped.

"Then why were you looking underneath the chairs? And you opened the lid of that trash can," the woman shook her head.

"She likes to play hide and seek!" Maude explained.

The woman simply stared at Maude, still looking very confused. Before Maude could say anything else, she walked off shaking her head.

"Opal Tyler, we need you to come to your gate to board your flight. Opal Tyler, please report to your gate immediately," a loud voice boomed.

"That should help," Ruby said breathlessly. "Do you see her?"

"No," Maude replied. "She's not over here anywhere. I looked under all the seats and in the trash cans. Where else could she be?"

"What are we going to do?" asked Ruby anxiously.

"We better hurry up and get on that plane before it leaves without us!" Maude huffed.

"Maude! We can't leave her!" Ruby shrieked.

"Oh, I know it, but durn her!" Maude growled. "This is just like her. Air travel has not been kind to us Ruby. Don't you forget that."

"Wait a minute, there she is!" Ruby squealed. "Opal, over here! Opal!"

Maude could just make out Opal walking slowly through the crowd. "Hurry up," she added loudly.

As Opal got closer, Maude saw a look of amazement on her face. "Where have you been?" Maude asked, while jerking her arm towards the plane.

"Did you hear it?" Opal asked.

"Hear what?" Maude asked.

"It sounded like God," Opal breathed.

"The voice telling you to hurry up and board the airplane that's been waiting on you?" Maude gasped.

"Yes," said Opal. She turned to Ruby for confirmation.

Round Trip

"That was the gate agent telling you to hurry up! We don't have all day Opal. You near about got left behind!" Maude sighed. "Now get a move on!" She steered Opal down the aisle and plopped her down in the first empty seat between two sharply dressed men in black suits. "Don't move a muscle, I swear to everything that's holy."

Maude turned to see Ruby behind her red-faced. "What's your problem?" she asked her.

"Everyone is staring at us!" Ruby whispered.

"Aren't you used to that by now?" Maude sighed. "Come on! There's two empty seats near the back. At least I'm close to the restroom."

Ruby sat in the middle seat next to a young man covered in tattoos who smiled at them both. Maude took the aisle seat and immediately looked around for the paper air sickness bags.

Rain hit the window as the plane started to edge forward. During their hour layover inside, a storm had blown over the airport.

"Is it safe to fly in the rain? Was that thunder?" Maude howled.

"It's safe," the tattooed man assured her. "You won't even notice it once we're up there."

Ruby returned his smile and jumped into a conversation about gardening once she saw his rose tattoo on his forearm. Maude couldn't find the bags she needed and barreled to the restroom behind her instead.

"Is she ok?" the man asked.

"No," Ruby answered. "But there's nothing we can do about that."

"Hi!" Opal exclaimed. She plopped down in the seat next to Ruby and smiled. "I'm Opal!"

"Hi, I'm Mark," the man smiled. "And this is Mrs. Ruby."

"Oh, I've known Ruby since we were knee high to grasshoppers," Opal laughed. "Where'd Maude run off to?"

Ruby pointed over her head to the restroom and shrugged. "You know how she gets."

"I do," nodded Opal solemnly. "If she'd only try some of my motion sickness supplements, but hey, what do I know?"

Opal, Ruby, and Mark launched into a pleasant conversation about herbal remedies while Maude tried to steady herself in the restroom. When she finally came out, she found Opal in her seat drawing on her arms with a black marker.

"What in the devil are you doing?" she hissed.

"Mark and I are discussing the benefits of plant-based ink," Opal said matter of factly.

"Who's Mark?" Maude asked.

"Hi, I'm Mark," the man smiled. "And I've heard all about you."

"Of course you have," sighed Maude.

"Ma'am, I need you to take your seat please," the flight attendant said.

"Opal, move back to your seat," Maude said.

"I don't want to," said Opal. "It was so boring up there. No one would talk to me. The man on my left kept snoring and the man on my right was reading some boring magazine. It's so much more fun back here!"

"Opal," begged Maude.

"How about I switch seats with you?" Mark offered. "That way you three can sit together and talk about your trip," he winked.

"That is so sweet! Thank you," Ruby smiled.

"Aw, you've been so much fun to talk to," Opal sulked. She shook his hand and said she'd be in touch.

"What? Did y'all exchange phone numbers or something?" Maude asked.

"We sure did," Opal nodded. "There's always room for a business connection, even on a pleasure trip."

"That just sounds weird," Maude muttered. "Now scoot on over so I can sit on the outside."

Ruby and Opal shifted over a seat so Maude could sit by the aisle in case her anxiety reared its ugly head again.

"I love sitting by the window," Ruby said. "Everything looks like ants down below."

"What a great metaphor for life," Opal exclaimed. "It's all about perspective."

Maude rolled her eyes and held on tightly to the armrest. "Now ain't the time for a philosophical lecture."

"I know you don't understand metaphors," Opal said. "Just keep holding on and don't think about all that pizza and wine and bagels and Chinese food waiting for us when we land!"

"Ugh," moaned Maude. She jumped up out of her seat and crammed herself in the bathroom.

"Opal! That wasn't nice," Ruby said. "But maybe Mark will come back! He was such a sweet young man."

"I thought you didn't like tattoos," Opal raised her eyebrows in mock concern.

"I only said I didn't want any tattoos. But I can appreciate them on somebody else," Ruby blushed.

"Especially if that somebody is tanned and muscled," Opal agreed.

"Opal! I'm a married woman. And you're, well, you have a gentleman caller," Ruby grinned.

"Looking doesn't hurt anyone," Opal smiled. "Jameson and Mortie will understand. The way that boy looks, they'd be appreciating him, too!"

"You are too much," laughed Ruby. "Can you picture Jameson or Mortie with tattoos?"

"Heavens no!" laughed Opal. "Well, maybe. Now that I think about it, a nice set of skulls might be what Mortie needs. He needs some color in his wardrobe, so why not on his skin? You know he rarely gets outside in his line of work."

Ruby shook her head and laughed. "Jameson would never. Maybe if Mortie does first. Then again, the hold you have over that man, he might get a whole back piece if you asked him."

"Oh stop," Opal said. "It's not like that."

"He adores you," Ruby continued. "It's nice to see. Ever think about settling down one of these days?"

"Not a chance," Opal said. "Mortie is wonderful. He's calm and sweet, and so genuine, but I don't want to get married. I don't think he does either. We both have such busy, fulfilling lives. He's never asked and neither have I. I like it like that."

"I'm glad you're happy. Speaking of marriage proposals, I heard that Eddie Walker asked Maureen to marry him," Ruby said. She raised her eyebrows and looked at Opal squarely.

"It's about time," Opal said. "I love Eddie, I really do, but he's a lot to handle. He's preciously sweet, but it's sometimes too much. He still sends me flowers on my birthday, the salon's anniversary, and for the summer and winter solstice."

"Y'all broke up over a year ago," gasped Ruby.

"I know," Opal said. "He's just a sweetheart. I hated to break up with him, but after declining his marriage proposal three different times, I knew there was no other way for him to understand. Maureen is such a nice woman. She's always in and out of the flower shop and the Comb Over. I think they'll both be happy together."

Ruby nodded. "Any plans to see Ricky while we're up here?"

Ricky McNeal was another one of Opal's boyfriends from a few years ago. Ricky was an expert seamstress, avid theatre goer, and could dance on a dime. He added an aura of eccentric fun and thrill to Rhinestone. Opal was crushed when he decided to close up his shop and move back home to New York City two years ago in the spring of 1987.

"We talked on the phone last week," Opal smiled. "Unfortunately, he won't be in town while we're there. His show closed last weekend and he took some time off before the next one. He and his roommate are going on a cruise to the Bahamas to celebrate a successful show run," Opal beamed.

"Oh, I know that's disappointing for you," Ruby patted her hand. "I know you've missed seeing him."

"Yes, but he seems so happy," Opal smiled. "He and Paolo adopted two cats and have a cute little studio apartment together. Sounds like a dream."

"It sure does," smiled Ruby.

"But he told me all of the fun places to go," Opal assured her. "There's this perfect nightclub he said I would absolutely love! We have to go. He said Cher is performing this week."

"Cher?" Ruby gasped.

"Yes! All kinds of celebrities go there. Ricky knows all the ends and outs of New York. He wanted to make sure we didn't stick out like tourists;" Opal continued.

"Good idea," agreed Ruby. "Oh Maude, are you feeling better?"

Maude had sunk down in the seat next to Opal looking a little less green than she had looked. "I think so," she whispered.

"We were just talking about seeing Cher while we're in New York. Ricky's told Opal where she'll be performing this week," Ruby explained.

"I love Cher," Maude nodded. "Are you sure?"

"Oh yes," nodded Opal. "Cher, and Barbra, too."

"Barbra who?" Maude asked.

"Streisand, of course!" laughed Opal. "Who else could it be?"

"Wow!" exclaimed Ruby and Maude together.

"I think we must be getting ready to land. I can't believe we're in New York City!" Ruby cheered. "This is going to be the best trip ever."

Maude nodded, but clenched the armrest as the plane turned over the water below. "If I survive," she grimaced.

Opal applauded loudly as soon as the wheels touched the pavement. She could barely contain her excitement. Ruby was not far behind her. She jumped up and grabbed her purse and hurried behind Opal who had already stepped over Maude in her seat.

"They haven't told us that we can get off the plane yet," Maude pointed out.

"We have a lot of ground to cover," Opal countered. "You chose to sit in the last row, not me."

Maude rolled her eyes and slowly stood up to try and keep her balance. She flung her purse and the bag of snacks Ruby had purchased her over her shoulder and gave Ruby a gentle shove forward.

"Ow, Maude!" Ruby exclaimed. "There's nowhere to go yet!"

"That's what I tried to tell you, but y'all were so gung-ho to jump up!" Maude frowned.

She sat back down in her seat and waited for the line to start moving. When it finally did, she followed Ruby and Opal down the aisle. Opal high-fived the pilot on the way out which made him smile broadly. Maude rolled her eyes, but she had to appreciate the childlike joy that Opal brought to most situations. Plus, she was finally in New York City with her two best friends.

๑Chapter Six๑

After they found their luggage at baggage claim, Opal showed them how to hail a cab in front of the airport doors. She was an expert when it came to flagging down cars and men, so Maude and Ruby stood back on the corner and laughed at her theatrics. It only took thirty seconds before two yellow taxi cabs pulled up to the curb. Opal flashed her best smile and held the door open for Maude to climb in the back after they loaded their suitcases into the trunk. Once Ruby climbed in after her, Opal shut the door and hopped in the front of the cab with the driver.

"To the Plaza," she yelled triumphantly.

Martin may have skimped when it came to the airlines, but he made sure the women spared no expense when it came to the hotel. The Plaza in New York City was considered the most luxurious, grandest hotel in all of the world, at least according to his agent friends from up north. He assured Maude, Opal, and Ruby that they would be more than satisfied with their suite near Central Park.

When Maude stepped out of the cab and began walking up the steps, she was greeted by a doorman dressed in his best attire.

"How can I help you?" he asked.

"Is this the Plaza?" Maude asked.

"Yes, it is," he answered.

"This is the right place, Ruby. Martin sure did good with this one," Maude called over her shoulder.

Apparently, the doorman recognized the name Martin from somewhere else. "Oh, you're with Martin's group? That explains it. The service entrance is around the corner. You're a little early though. His people normally don't show up for another few hours, but that's not a problem. We have a lot to prepare for this evening."

"Why do we need the service entrance?" Maude stood back.

"Well, that's where service people enter. This must be your first assignment. Honestly, he normally picks his girls from a different age bracket," the doorman clarified under his breath. "But we need all hands on deck for this wedding."

"What do you mean age bracket?" Maude huffed.

"Well, I," he stammered.

"I think there's been a misunderstanding. We're here for a vacation. Our travel agent, Martin Rhodes, booked us a room here," Ruby offered.

"Oh, I'm sorry, madam. We have a contractor named Martin who sends a lot of workers to the hotel," the doorman quickly apologized. "Right this way," he held the door open for the three ladies.

"What did he mean a different age bracket?" Maude continued to fume.

"Hush Maude," Opal said. "Honestly, you're going to get us kicked out before we even check in."

"He called me old and he said I looked like I was going to work. This is my best outfit," Maude huffed. She was clearly outdone with this man's behavior.

Opal looked Maude up and down. "Yeah, we probably need to do something about that. You've never been stylish like me and Ruby."

"Oh my goodness! Can you believe this lobby?" Ruby changed the subject quickly.

The Plaza Hotel was an icon of New York City with numerous wealthy and famous guests. Weddings, balls, benefits, and conferences from all over the world were held at the Plaza. The Plaza Hotel has appeared in numerous books and films, and was listed as a National Historic Landmark. Ruby had instantly been enamored with the idea of staying at The Plaza. One of her favorite movies, starring Barbra Streisand, was filmed there. She felt like a movie star the moment she entered the lobby.

"This is the fanciest place I've ever seen," she whispered in awe. "They don't have hotels like this in Rhinestone."

The hustle and bustle of the gorgeous hotel was almost too much to take in. Ruby clutched her hand to her mouth numerous times in amazement. Even Maude was taken in by the grandeur of things.

"I'll check us in while you two marvel," Opal smiled. "But don't touch anything, Maude."

"I wasn't going to," Maude snapped, as she pulled her hand back from the column she had been reaching out to touch.

Opal laughed and skipped off towards the line of people waiting to check in.

"This is amazing," Ruby continued. "I almost don't want to leave the lobby! I wonder if we'll see anyone famous! Oh my heavens, what if we do?"

"We'll act normal," Maude instructed. "Well, as normal as we can be. Hell, Opal already thinks she's famous everywhere she goes, so just be yourself. I'll be myself and Opal will just have to be whatever character she's in the mood to be."

Ruby nodded and continued to look around the lobby. "This is so fancy," she said again.

As soon as Opal had them checked in, she found Ruby and Maude staring out one of the front windows.

"Isn't this grand?" Opal asked with a wave of her hand. "Honestly, this is really the life I was born for, although I greatly prefer the simpler things."

"Says the one who spends all her free time out digging up weeds in every patch of woods near Rhinestone," Maude huffed.

"I do that to maintain my connection with nature and all living things, but I definitely could have made it big here if I'd chosen Broadway over beauty," Opal replied. "It's a calling, you know. The women of

91

Rhinestone need me more than the Big Apple, I'm afraid. You should know that most of all, Maude."

"What do you mean by that?" Maude huffed. "I can do just fine with my bottle of Pert from the Piggly Wiggly."

"My point exactly. You need me more than you'll ever know," Opal agreed. "Now, the gentleman at the counter said the elevators are this way," Opal held out her arm toward the right. "Shall we?"

"Don't go getting all uppity, Opal Tyler. I know where you sleep, remember?" Maude said.

"How can I forget? Neighbors can hear you snoring from a block away," Opal said cheerfully.

Before Maude could respond, Opal weaved her way through the crowd of people gathering in the lobby. She was holding the door open for her friends when they caught up with her.

"Twelfth floor please," Opal asked the man who stepped in after they did.

Ruby nudged Maude and quickly motioned with her eyes at the man beside them. Maude's mouth fell open.

"Is it?" Maude mouthed to Ruby.

"I don't know," Ruby whispered back.

Opal had begun a full conversation with the man in question. When the doors opened up on the twelfth floor, the three ladies stepped out into the brightly lit hallway. The man waved goodbye to Opal and her friends and continued his elevator ride up.

"Oh my heavens, Opal. Did you just have a conversation with JFK, Jr.?" Ruby squealed.

Opal stared at her friend. "Of course not, Ruby. Everyone knows John Jr. doesn't live in a hotel."

"I swear that was him," Maude said breathlessly.

"It's really a good thing that I'm here with you both. Otherwise, Maude would have you both going up to every random stranger asking if they were famous," Opal sighed. She turned and headed down the hallway toward their room.

"I swear that was him," Maude whispered to Ruby.

"It sure looked like him, but if anyone would know these things, it's Opal," Ruby said.

"Opal doesn't know. She thinks she's the most famous person alive," Maude said.

"Well, she is probably the most famous person to come out of Rhinestone," Ruby offered.

"Don't tell her that. She already has an ego the size of three counties," Maude mumbled.

They found Opal halfway down the hall, standing in front of an opened door.

"Will y'all hurry up? You're spending half the day wandering the halls," Opal told them.

"Oh my goodness, this room is enormous," Ruby gushed. She set her bags down on the nearest bed and looked around. She scurried to the window and gasped. "This view is amazing."

Maude flung her bags down on the chair and met Ruby by the window. "Martin really outdid himself with this one. This must be the nicest place in town."

"This is definitely a step up from the last place I stayed," Opal agreed.

"I don't even want to know," Maude replied. "Okay, let's hurry up and get ready for dinner. I'm starving."

"You're always hungry," Opal replied. "Comb your hair and we'll get you fed."

"What's wrong with my hair?" Maude asked.

"Oh Maude, maybe you should just wear this instead," Opal offered her a hat from her bag.

"Maude doesn't need to wear a hat," Ruby said. "Let's just go. I can't wait to explore the city."

"Race you to the elevator!" Opal shouted over her shoulder.

"One minute she's trying to be all sophisticated, and the next minute she's acting like a twelve-year-old kid," Maude mumbled as she shut the door behind them. "Wait for me!"

"I swear, you two!" Ruby shook her head. She doubled her walk to catch them at the elevators. "You know, even the hallways are nice," Ruby admired.

"Sure beats those rooms we stayed in when we went to Italy, doesn't it?" Maude laughed.

"The one with the terrible picture of the ocean?" Ruby laughed.

"That's the one! Ocean view, my tail!" Maude huffed.

"We don't want a view of that either, thanks," Opal quipped.

"Y'all stop! This is a respectable place," Ruby warned. The elevator dinged and the doors opened.

"Anyone famous in here?" Opal asked before stepping inside. The three people in the elevator merely stared back at them. "Ok, looks like we're good," Opal grinned back at Maude and Ruby who both looked embarrassed.

No one said anything during the ride down to the lobby. Once they were back in the lobby, Opal yawned and stretched her arms over her head. "Ok, what's for supper?" she asked.

"Pizza," Maude said without hesitation.

"Works for me," shrugged Opal. "Let's grab a few slices and walk through Central Park."

"Or we could sit down at a restaurant and I can get off these feet," Maude suggested.

"Get off your feet? You've been sitting in a car and an airplane all day," Ruby laughed.

"I carry all my stress in my feet," Maude explained.

"That explains a lot," Opal nodded. "They're the size of canoes!"

Ruby shushed them before they could get any further. "Come on you two. You are not going to embarrass me in New York City. It's too fancy of a city to be acting like that. We weren't raised in a barn!"

The wind was chilly when they exited the doors of the hotel. They wrapped their coats tighter around them and marveled at the crowds of people passing by. If they weren't careful, they too would be caught in the whirlwind.

Opal hailed another cab and jumped in the front seat with the unsuspecting driver. Maude and Ruby piled into the backseat and waited for Opal to tell the driver where to go.

"Take us to the best place for real New York pizza," Opal instructed.

"The best?" he repeated. "You got it!"

Without looking behind him, he took off and swerved around the cars in front of him. Ruby stared out of the window with childlike glee while Maude held her hand to her mouth.

"Shouldn't you slow down?" she howled.

"Huh?" the driver asked.

"You're driving like a crazy person!" Maude yelped.

Ruby turned her attention to Maude and laughed. "Reminded me of your driving actually."

Maude rolled her eyes and breathed a sigh of relief as the taxi slammed on brakes. They were stopped in front of a rundown looking building with a neon red sign in the window that boasted of pizza and sandwiches.

"This place?" Maude asked.

"Best pie in the world," the driver nodded.

"I don't want pie. I want pizza," Maude frowned.

"Pizza pie," he snorted. "You's must not be from around here." His snickering aggravated Maude, but before she could retort, Ruby thanked him and helped Maude out of the car.

Opal was already inside the building sitting at the counter on a rickety bar stool. "It smells so good in here," she exclaimed.

The woman behind the counter nodded and asked what she would like to order.

"Three sweet teas and a large pepperoni pizza," Maude interrupted.

"We don't have sweet tea," the woman smirked. "We got pop."

"Whatever you have is fine," Ruby countered. "Maude, stop it. You're making us sound like bumpkins. You have to blend."

"Half cheese, half pepperoni," Opal added. "No meat for me."

"Blend? Like blend in?" Maude grumbled. "Opal's wearing a shirt with glitter and rhinestones on it, Ruby. We don't blend!"

"Hush! People are staring again," Ruby whispered.

"You might as well get over that," Opal laughed. "If Maude's not causing a scene, she's not truly happy." Opal laughed and turned back to the woman behind the counter who was staring impatiently at the trio.

"Anyway, cheese and half pepperoni pizza is fine. Thank you," she smiled at the woman who shrugged and turned back towards the kitchen.

She returned a few minutes later with three glasses, three soda cans, and three plates. "It'll be about fifteen minutes. I'll bring out the pizza when it's ready."

While Opal spun around on the stool at the counter, Maude and Ruby wandered around the small pizza shop. The decor was different than anything they had ever seen before. Black and white photos of burly men tossing pizzas in the air were framed on the dingy wall below a map of Italy.

"It's so dirty in here, but it smells amazing," Maude whispered loudly.

"Maude, you talk too loud! People will hear you. Come on, let's go back and sit with Opal," Ruby said quickly. She led Maude back to the counter and sat next to Opal.

When the pizza was brought to their table a few minutes later, Maude's eyes widened in surprise. The steaming melted cheese dropped off the sides of the pan and the pepperoni looked crisp.

"Maybe this is what Heaven looks like," Maude swallowed. "I think I'm in love."

"It does look good," nodded Opal.

"Shh, I just need to savor this moment," Maude shushed her.

"Do you have any forks or a knife?" Ruby asked the woman.

"No," the woman behind the counter shook her head. "You don't eat it with a fork."

"Right," Ruby smiled. She turned towards Opal and asked quietly, "how do I eat it then?"

"You fold it," the woman explained. She stared at the three women and shook her head slightly before waking back to the kitchen.

"I'll show you," Opal said. She pulled one of the large slices apart and watched the cheese stretch. "Then you just bend it, fold it in half. Like this!"

Opal folded her side of pizza like a taco and bit into it. "This is good!"

"Where you guys from?" the woman couldn't help herself from asking.

"Rhinestone!" Ruby replied with a bit more enthusiasm than she had intended.

"Rhinestone?" the woman asked callously. "Like the crystal stuff?"

"Exactly," nodded Opal. "Second only to diamonds!"

"Rhinestone is a city just a little south of here," smiled Ruby.

"A little south?" Maude repeated? "Ruby, it's over a thousand miles south!"

"I'm sure," nodded the woman. "I could tell by your accent that you wasn't from around here."

"Accent? We ain't the ones with accents," hiccupped Maude. "Y'all the ones who talk funny up here."

"Maude!" stammered Ruby. "Be nice!"

"Well, it's true," Maude finished. "I don't even know half of what they're saying."

The woman merely smirked and yelled over her shoulder. "Hey Tony! This broad says you talk funny!"

A large man, presumably Tony, walked through the curtain. He wiped his flour-stained hands on his pants and chuckled. "Oh yea? Who says?"

Opal and Ruby both pointed their fingers at Maude who had taken another big bite of pizza.

"I talk funny?" he asked.

"Yea," said Maude, her mouth still full of pizza.

"Maude, sit down and stop!" Ruby blushed. She turned to the man behind the counter and shook her head. "She's all bark," she smiled.

"Where'd you say they were from, Maria?" Tony asked.

"Down south," Maria smiled. "I knew you'd want to meet them."

"I do love a good southern accent!" Tony grinned. "You don't get much of that up here. Never been down south, but I think it's real cute."

Ruby blushed again and Opal smiled radiantly. "Well, I do declare," she giggled. "It's not every day that we meet such a fine, young gentleman," she cooed.

"Opal, knock it off!" Maude grumbled. "You don't sound like that. This ain't a game!"

Tony and Maria were in heaven with Opal's theatrics. They each asked her to say random words and lapped it all up. Ruby smiled along gracefully while Maude grumbled to herself. Once the pizza was finished, she drained her glass and paid the bill.

"Are y'all coming?" she bellowed from the doorway.

"Oh, yes, we are ready. Thank y'all so much for your charming hospitality. We do appreciate all the wonderful things you've shared with us. Don't be a stranger, dear. Tata," Opal waved goodbye dramatically. She and Ruby exited the door and followed Maude to the street corner.

"What in the world was all that?" Maude demanded. "This ain't the theatre."

"All the world's a stage, Maude. And I'm a darn good actress," Opal grinned.

~Chapter Seven~

Maude stretched and yawned loudly early the next morning. She was surprised to see Ruby and Opal still asleep. Usually, she was the last among the trio to rise each morning when they were on vacation. Opal rarely slept as it was. She said she had too much life left to live, or something like that. Maude figured it was best not to wake them. Jet lag was real and they would need all of their energy for the adventures over the next few days. She sat up on the side of the bed and stretched again.

"Good grief. Do you make that much noise every morning?" Opal asked her without lifting her head from the pillow.

"I didn't say anything," Maude said.

"No, but your body did. Every bone in your body popped and crackled," Opal said. "That's not a good sign."

"Can't help it. I have to get limbered up in the mornings," Maude said, twisting around and causing a loud snapping sound from her lower back.

"Next time remind me to bring a can of oil," Opal said, sitting up and yawning. "Or at least some WD40."

"If it'd work, I'd be willing to try it," Maude stretched in the other direction.

"So, does that mean you'll be willing to try my new joint and muscle cream? I'm coming out with an entirely new line designed to keep the older population of Rhinestone in tiptop condition," Opal offered.

"What do you mean older?" Maude stared at her.

"Well, you are getting up there," Opal began. "You're what we like to call an antique."

"We're all getting up there," Maude replied.

"Yes, but some of us are getting there a little bit faster than the other two," Opal said, standing up and reaching to the skies. "And by some of us, I mean you."

"We're the same age," Maude huffed.

"Not exactly. You are significantly older than I am," Opal bent down to touch her toes.

"Significantly?" Maude said. "I'm three months older than you. By that logic, Ruby should be in a walker."

"Four months," sighed Opal. "Math was never your strong suit."

"And I'm only the oldest by two weeks, Maude. That doesn't count," Ruby joined the conversation without lifting her head off the pillow. "Not even two weeks. More like twelve days."

"Besides, you were born older, Maude," Opal said. She spread her arms wide and lunged forward, almost touching her back knee to the ground. "Maybe not maturity wise, but health wise."

"Born older?" Maude stood up quickly. "Opal Tyler, I swear one of these days you are going to push me to my absolute limit! And stop doing that bendy thing. You're making me dizzy!" She grabbed some clothes from her suitcase and headed to the bathroom for her shower.

"If she'd do more of these bendy things, she wouldn't make as many noises in the morning," Opal said, now lunging with the other leg.

"She's not the only one who makes a lot of noise when she wakes up. Seems like my knees are always stiff in the mornings," Ruby laughed. "This getting old business is not for sissies."

"I can show you some simple things to help with that. You're still in the prime of life," Opal told her. "You're aging like fine wine."

"Then what about Maude?" Ruby smiled.

"Oh, you know, Maude. She ages more like vinegar," Opal said. She was once again touching her toes.

By the time Maude stepped out of the bathroom, Ruby and Opal were almost ready to go.

"I'm hungry," Maude said. "All this talk about age has my stomach growling."

"Let's get bagels and lox for you two, and a plain bagel with butter for me," Opal offered.

"Sounds fishy," Maude said with her nose wrinkled.

"Exactly," said Opal. "You'll love it. There's carts sprinkled all throughout the park, I'm sure."

Before Maude could protest, Opal bounded out of the elevator and made her way to the front door. The lobby was a whirlwind, but in order to keep up with Opal, Maude and Ruby couldn't take the time to look around. Opal was already outside chatting with the doorman by the time they walked outside.

"Just as I suspected," she smiled at Maude and Ruby. "The best bagel cart is right across the street." She bowed to the doorman and followed the crowd of people who were walking across the street.

"I swear, half my life is spent chasing after this woman," Maude mumbled to Ruby. They hurried behind Opal who wasn't easy to miss in the crowd. Opal had donned her best purple pantsuit, complete with a feathery boa around her shoulders. They weren't sure why she insisted on carrying a faux-leather briefcase with her, but knew it was best not to ask many questions. Opal had always danced to the beat of her own drum.

"Over here!" Opal called out. She had found a cart that had a handwritten sign boasting of the best bagels in New York. While Opal ordered their breakfast, Maude and Ruby looked around for somewhere to get a cup of coffee to no avail.

"Here you go," Opal said. She held out two wrapped bagels towards Ruby and Maude. "Let's go sit on these cute little benches over there."

"I need some coffee," Maude yawned. "Where's the coffee cart?"

"We're in New York City, the options are endless," Opal smiled. "Finish your bagel and we'll find a cute little coffee shop on our way to the water."

"I can't wait to see the Statue of Liberty," Ruby added. "I bet it's even bigger in person."

"It's a pretty steady climb, from what I hear," Opal explained. "Think we can make it up?"

"I am not about to try and climb the outside of the Statue of Liberty," Maude huffed.

"I meant to climb the stairs on the inside. Honestly, Maude, sometimes you can be so uncouth!" Opal said, shaking her head.

Ruby nodded and looked earnestly at Maude. "I think we can. Might take us a minute, but just imagine the view!"

They finished their bagels quickly and followed the instructions from the bagel cart owner to the nearest coffee shop. Maude threw back two small cups of strong black coffee before letting Opal step outside to flag down a taxi to take them to where they could board the ferry to Liberty Island.

Battery Park was crawling with people. While Ruby purchased their tickets for the next ferry, Opal and Maude walked along the shoreline watching people. The Statue of Liberty was visible from where they were standing, but Maude couldn't get her camera to focus just right.

"We have about fifteen minutes before our trip," Ruby said. She handed them each a ticket and pulled her coat closer to her body. The wind coming off of the water was chilly.

"Look at those statues over yonder," Maude pointed out. "I swear one of them moved a second ago." She rubbed her eyes and blinked hard.

"Statues don't move," Ruby shook her head.

"I know that, but I swear! Did you see that! That one moved!" Maude cried.

"Seeing things again," Opal lamented. "Come on Ruby, you get on one side of her and I'll get on the other. The last thing we need is for Maude to fall into the water."

"I'm not seeing things and I ain't gonna fall overboard," Maude retorted. "Those aren't real statues, I'm telling you."

"There, there, Maude. It's okay. We'll take care of you," Opal patted Maude's arm gently. "Honestly, we may need to have someone start looking after you when we get back home. They say the mind is the first thing to go."

"If you don't get your hands off of me, I swear I'm going to," Maude yanked her arm away quickly.

Ruby pushed between them and guided Maude toward the water. "Let's walk closer to the ferry," Ruby said. "We can be some of the first ones on!"

They walked closer to where the ferry was docked. A crowd had gathered around a female statue that changed positions right in front of their eyes. "See! I told you!" snapped Maude.

"Well, to be fair, it's a street performer, not a statue," Ruby mentioned.

"It still moved!" Maude reiterated. "Anyway, they're boarding now. Let's go!"

She led the way towards the ferry and handed her ticket to the man by the ramp. Rub and Opal handed over their tickets and followed Maude up the ramp. They weren't the first onboard, but there were still plenty of seats to choose from. Ruby chose the bench close to the front of the ferry and sat down. "We have the perfect view," she shrieked happily.

As soon as the ferry began to move through the water, Maude's stomach began to churn. Water travel was also not her preferred method of travel. With each lurch of the boat, the bagels and coffee threatened to make a dramatic return. She closed her eyes and ignored the shrieks and excited gasps from either side of her as they inched closer to the landmark. Once her feet were back on solid ground, she inhaled deeply and exhaled loudly.

"Ok, I think I'm ready now," she whispered through gritted teeth.

"Great! Because there's hundreds of steps to climb," Opal smiled.

Maude rolled her eyes, but followed dutifully behind Opal and Ruby who both seemed to skip merrily in the morning breeze. The climb took almost thirty minutes to get to the last step. Maude supposed that it would have taken half the time if Ruby had not stopped every few feet to marvel at the thought of being inside one of the most historical landmarks.

"Yes, Ruby, we know! Now keep moving or the folks behind me are going to start shoving again!" Maude hissed.

The view from the crown was phenomenal. They couldn't help but hold their breath as they snapped continuous pictures of the water below them and the skyline ahead.

After a quick lunch of hotdogs from a street cart, the three friends jumped in a taxi cab to visit The Metropolitan Museum of Art.

"The Metropolitan," sighed Opal dreamily. "It sounds so fancy because it truly is. Now, there are some ground rules. No touching. No stealing. Don't even stare too hard or too long. It's disrespectful."

"Disrespectful? To the artwork?" Ruby gasped. "Thank you for telling us, Opal. We don't want to do that," she added seriously.

"How can you be disrespectful to a piece of paper or a rock?" Maude guffawed.

"Maude! Don't say things like that!" Ruby exclaimed.

"A rock? A piece of paper? Oh Maude, it's worse than I ever thought," Opal shook her head.

"What are you going on about?" demanded Maude.

"Your lack of culture," Opal clarified. "I've been hoping that these last forty plus years of being in my presence would have rubbed off on you, but I see that I was wrong. It's sad really," she sighed.

Ruby shook her head and agreed with Opal. Maude, instead, rolled her eyes and walked up the steps towards the museum. "You two are deranged," she said over her shoulder. "Now hurry up or I'll make sure to stare extra hard and make it awkward. I might even try to touch one of the frames."

Opal shrieked. "You wouldn't dare!"

"Maude Cooper!" exclaimed Ruby.

Maude smirked seeing the exasperation on their faces. "Hmm. We'll see," she turned away so they wouldn't see the broad smile across her face and marched to the entrance.

Ruby and Opal followed behind her, still shaking their heads as they passed through the doors that held musical instruments, historical artifacts, costumes, and priceless paintings from all over the world. Opal said she could feel the history when she stood near the artwork, but Maude rebuffed her and said she didn't believe in that hullabaloo, though Ruby again agreed with Opal.

"Their collection includes pieces from Vermeer, Rembrandt, Caravaggio, and Raphael," explained Opal. "That's amazing."

"Those sound like diseases," gagged Maude.

"You are so unrefined! Those men are some of the greatest minds the world will ever know," Opal sassed back.

"Opal, I've seen some better art on the backsides of barns in Rhinestone. Now I'll admit, some of this stuff is beautiful, but some of it looks like trash," Maude countered.

"Y'all stop," Ruby hissed. "I swear, I can't take y'all anywhere. This is a respectable place. Maude, act right. Opal, you can't make her like art the way that we do." Ruby adjusted her purse on her shoulder and walked off, leaving Opal and Maude in her wake.

"Look what you did," Opal said. "Upsetting Ruby like that."

Before Maude could retort, Opal sashayed off behind Ruby and began pointing out random facts about the collection she wanted to see on the second floor. It could take days to see everything that they wanted to see, but they only had the afternoon due to their packed itinerary. Opal and Ruby hurried through as many areas of the museum as they could and found Maude in the exhibit featuring decorative art from the reign of King Louis XIV.

"Not too shabby," Maude said aloud to the man next to her. He shrugged his shoulders and turned back to his wife who looked annoyed. "I was talking about the tapestry," Maude snapped.

"Making friends again, I see," Opal said as she appeared from nowhere in time to see the wife tugging violently on her husband's arm.

"I was just trying to be neighborly," Maude said, a bit outdone by the couple's rudeness.

"We really need to work on your social skills. You could be a nice person if you tried a little harder," Opal told her.

"Y'all!" Ruby elbowed her. "Don't be ugly."

"What is that supposed to mean?" Maude demanded.

Opal hummed knowingly before changing the subject. "Ready to go?" Opal asked.

"I've been ready. I've been waiting on you two," Maude said. "Where are we eating tonight? I'm starving!"

"Ruby and I picked Chinese food," Opal responded.

"Fine," Maude grumbled.

They made their way to the main entrance. Ruby and Opal stopped a few times along the way to admire a few pieces they had missed earlier. By the time they made it to the corner, the wind had picked up considerably. Thankfully, Opal was able to flag down a cab within a few minutes. She jumped into the front seat before the driver could say anything.

He stared at her with a cigarette dangling from his mouth. "Where to?" he mumbled.

"Chinatown!" Opal told him.

"I thought that was a movie," Maude whispered to Ruby who only shrugged in response.

"Right," the man grunted. He stomped on the gas pedal and whipped into traffic without glancing in either direction.

"Prepare for takeoff!" Opal squealed.

Maude and Ruby tried to brace themselves for the rollercoaster ride through the streets of New York.

"Is he driving with his eyes closed?" Maude demanded.

"Easier that way," the driver grumbled in response.

"Oh sweet Lord Jesus, we're gonna die!" Maude said, holding onto the back of the front seat for dear life.

When Maude finally opened her eyes, they were driving into a completely different area of the city. All the signs were written in Chinese letters with English subtitles.

"It's like we drove into another country," Ruby said.

"This isn't anything like the movie," Maude whispered. "And before you even start, Opal, I'm ordering my own food tonight. I know how you're always going on about changing my palette, or whatever you call it."

"May the odds be good to you," Opal said and crossed herself.

The cab pulled up to the curve. "We're here!" Opal sang. "Pay the man, Maude!" Opal and Ruby were on the sidewalk before Maude could respond.

Chapter Eight

"Oh, look at all these shops!" Ruby exclaimed as they walked through a sea of vendors and restaurants. Her eyes were as wide as saucers.

"Food first, Ruby. Then we can shop," Maude told her. Ruby always got a sudden burst of energy when she spotted a potential good deal. "Ruby!"

"But these scarves are so pretty!" Ruby had stopped to admire the rows of boxes set up in an informal display. "And look at those purses! I just can't decide which ones to get! This one looks more like your style. What do you think?"

"They don't look nearly as appetizing as that plate of sweet and sour pork I know they have over there,"

Maude told Ruby. She nudged Ruby's elbow and pointed to the restaurant across the street.

"Okay, we'll eat something, but then we really have to explore some of these shops afterwards. There's so much to choose from," Ruby said with a hint of hysteria that she normally got when surrounded by bargain deals.

Maude knew from experience that it was pointless to argue with Ruby when she was in the mood to shop. The only thing Maude could hope for was to eat before Ruby and Opal had her loaded down with excessive packages.

"Where's Opal?" Ruby asked. "I thought she was right behind us."

Maude spun around and looked behind her. "She was right here a second ago."

"Well she couldn't have gotten far," Ruby said as she craned her neck to look in every direction. "Right?"

"Couldn't have gotten far? This is Opal we're talking about. She could be on Broadway choreographing a show by now," Maude said. "I wouldn't put it past her!"

"She wouldn't have left Chinatown without us," Ruby sounded worried. "Right?"

"Of course not," Maude said. "She's probably somewhere showing everyone how to make paper dragons for the Chinese New Year."

"I don't think it's the right season for that," Ruby corrected her.

"Do you think that tidbit of information will stop Opal?" Maude asked.

Ruby nodded. "We better find her before she gets herself in trouble."

"Let's go this way," Maude took her by the elbow and dragged her off to the side where there was a break in the crowd.

"Do you think we should split up to cover more ground?" Ruby asked.

"No way. I'm not losing you, too!" Maude was adamant.

"You're right. We may never find each other again in this crowd," Ruby agreed.

"You think I'm joking about getting a tracker implanted in her. We need to get someone to invent a phone or something that you can carry around with you. Not that she'd be likely to answer it anyway!" Maude huffed. "We need some way to know where she is at all times."

"Who in the world wants a tracker, Maude?" Ruby looked at her. "That's got to be the craziest thing I've ever heard of."

"I don't care if it is. Opal needs one," Maude was firm. "I should have brought Buford's leash to wrap around her."

They jostled through the growing crowd from one booth to another. They looked in every store they passed. They scouted every restaurant, which only made Maude's stomach growl louder and more impatiently.

"Let's try this one," Maude instructed. They ducked their heads and entered a small, worn looking shop that was all but empty. "Oh! Never mind," Maude gagged. They hurried out just as quickly as they had entered.

"I don't know what they were cooking in that place, but let's not eat there," Ruby told Maude who had wrinkled her nose. Maude nodded in agreement.

After more than half an hour, Maude took Ruby's elbow and guided her into the mouth of a small alleyway.

"What are you doing?" Ruby asked, looking the length of the darkened alley. Boxes and rubbish were strewn about creating a series of eerie shadows along the buildings.

Maude turned and saw what Ruby was looking at. "Don't worry. I'm not crazy enough to go down there. I'm just trying to let some of the crowd pass by for a minute. But at this point, no one wants to mess with me. I'm half-starved and my feet are tired from walking."

"There must be a thousand people out here today," Ruby agreed.

"At least!" Maude agreed. "It's like looking for a needle in a haystack. An eccentric needle, but a needle nonetheless!"

They waited a few minutes until the bulk of the crowd had moved further up the street. Once Maude saw that the coast was clear, she took Ruby's elbow again and they stepped back out into the mayhem.

"Do you really think she could have gotten this far?" Ruby asked. "We've been looking for almost an hour."

"Yeah, but we've only gone a few blocks," Maude shrugged.

"Maybe she's looking for us back at those shops we were at," Ruby offered. "Maybe she doesn't know that she's lost!"

"Well, I think that's optimistic, but it sounds better than what we're doing," Maude agreed.

They turned back toward the direction they had originally come from. Walking against the crowd of people was worse than going with the flow. Finally they made it back to the shop Ruby had admired with all of the purses.

"I still say this one looks like something you'd carry," Ruby pointed out.

"Focus Ruby," Maude breathed.

"Sorry," Ruby said sheepishly. She sorted through a box of wallets and gasped. "This looks so fancy!"

"What? Ruby, the designer's name is misspelled!" Maude sighed. She rifled through the box in front of Ruby and shook her head. The bags were all wrapped in plastic and packaged haphazardly. "Ruby, you can't be serious."

Ruby's arms were loaded down with bags of all sizes. "We don't have these kinds in Rhinestone. They have an entirely different inventory here!"

"None of this is real!" Maude howled.

"Maude, don't say that!" Ruby shushed her.

"Hold on a second! Did you hear that?" Maude interrupted Ruby's rant about the price of handbags and certain authenticity.

Ruby paused and wrinkled her nose. "Did I hear what?"

"Over there!" Maude pointed towards the back of the small shop.

"What are you saying?" Ruby asked from over the pile of bags in her arms.

"Opal!" Maude called, ignoring Ruby's concern. "That's gotta be her!" She pushed through the racks of shawls and clothing towards the back of the shop.

"Maude, wait!" Ruby hurried behind her. She dropped her armful and pushed past the racks of clothes. "I can't see you! Ahh!" She slammed into Maude and shrieked. "What are you doing?"

"Shh! I swear I hear Opal laughing back there!" Maude repeated. She pressed her face against the thin door and listened intently. "I hear voices."

"Voices? You should talk to someone about that," Ruby said wide-eyed.

"Ruby hush! Listen," Maude instructed.

"I don't understand a word they're saying," Ruby shook her head.

"That! That laugh right there. That's Opal laughing," Maude said again.

"Maybe," Ruby added. "But I don't think they're speaking English."

"Oh, well, I think you're right," Maude sighed.

"Wait! I think that is Opal," said Ruby, pressing her ear harder against the door.

"But Opal doesn't speak Chinese," Maude reminded her.

Ruby raised her eyebrows and cocked her head. "I wouldn't be surprised, Maude. Opal has always surprised us with what she knows. She speaks Italian and Spanish. You know that's why she always orders for us at the Mexican restaurant."

"I know that, but Opal can't speak Chinese! Where in the world would she learn it!" Maude shouted.

Suddenly the door ripped open and Maude crumpled to the floor in a heap. Opal stood before them grinning. "Hey Ruby! I thought I heard Maude's dulcet tone out here. Where is she?"

Ruby's eye drifted immediately to the floor at Opal's feet. Maude reached her arm up and shouted, "Opal! What are you doing?"

"Maude! Get up off the floor for heaven's sake! We really can't take you anywhere. What are you doing down there? Come on," she sighed. She lifted Maude up to her feet and brushed her off.

"What are you doing in there?" Maude asked in a huff. "You just disappeared! What in the world!"

"I want you to meet my new friend," Opal said quickly, ignoring Maude's questions. "Come on in, Ruby." She ushered them both forward. A small woman wrapped in a colorful shawl smiled at them. "This is Min." Min bowed her head and kept smiling.

"Opal, what the heck are we doing here?" Maude whispered low.

"We've been talking about some natural additives for my Color Me Crazy line. She has so many secrets from the old world. She is such a treasure!" Opal smiled. Before Maude could reply, Opal jumped into an animated conversation in Mandarin with Min.

Ruby and Maude stared at each other in disbelief. They watched as Opal pulled out small sample bottles of her lotions, shampoos, creams, and elixirs and placed them on the table in between them. Min smiled and pulled off her colorful shawl and wrapped it around Opal's shoulders. The two women hugged and Opal bowed before turning back to Maude and Ruby. "Y'all about ready?"

"Ready? Ready for what? Opal, what in the sam hill!" Maude sputtered.

"I'm sure you're hungry," Opal continued. "Let's get some food in your belly before you waste away." She bellowed a hearty goodbye to Min who was busy smelling the contents on the bottles. Come on Maude, let's go Ruby. We don't want to overstay our welcome!"

Maude and Ruby allowed Opal to push them out of the room back through the racks and boxes of clothes and bags. Once they were back outside on the street, Ruby turned to Opal, still in disbelief.

"Opal, when did you learn to speak Chinese?" Ruby gasped.

"Mandarin," Opal corrected.

"Sounded like Chinese to me," Maude huffed.

"Chinese isn't a language, Maude. Everyone knows that," Opal shook her head in disbelief."

"Oh, ok," Ruby nodded. "Where did you learn Mandarin?"

"Opal, what in the world did you just do?" Maude demanded.

Opal flashed them a grin and pranced off towards the restaurant across the way.

"Opal! What planet is she from?" Maude turned and asked Ruby.

Ruby shrugged and linked arms with Maude. "As long as she comes in peace," Ruby giggled. "Come on, we better hurry up before we get lost again."

"We were never lost," Maude corrected. They hurried behind Opal who was already inside the restaurant. They found her sitting at a table near the front doors reading a piece of paper.

"There you both are! I was getting worried. Sit on down. I've already put in our orders," Opal explained.

Maude looked around and puffed up. "What? How? We were right behind you!"

"So, what have you two been up to?" Opal asked once Ruby and Maude sat down across from her.

"Us?" Maude howled.

"Yes, the two of you," Opal said slowly. "We may need to look into hearing aids for you, Maude. I'll ask Doctor Mead about it next time I take you over to Junction for your appointments. They have a nice, quaint little home across from the mall for senior citizens. Ruby and I can come visit you on Sundays for bingo," she said brightly.

"I swear," Maude growled through gritted teeth. "One of these days."

"Opal, what is going on?" Ruby interjected. "We thought we had lost you! Where have you been?"

"You saw where I was, Ruby," Opal said with a trace of concern in her voice. "I found you both behind that door in that shop not ten minutes ago. Did you hit your head or something?"

"Opal," begged Ruby. She too was starting to get impatient.

"Well, when you two wondered off, I saw these bottles on a shelf and had to investigate. Min and I got to talking and one thing led to another. We traded some insider secrets, and let me tell you, Rhinestone and ancient China aren't that different after all. Min is so sweet. She said if she's ever down in my neck of the woods, she'll look us up," Opal explained.

"Opal, you make friends everywhere you go," Ruby said in awe.

"I still want to know where you learned Chinese," Maude muttered.

"Crack open a book sometime, Maude," Opal responded. "The library is a vast wealth of knowledge. We'll take you to their children's reading program every Tuesday morning," she smirked. Before Maude could kick her under the table, the food was brought over in Styrofoam containers. "Smells amazing!" Opal smiled. She thanked the woman and handed Maude a pair of chopsticks. "Try not to stab at the food this time. Watch how Ruby and I do it."

Opal opened the containers and dished food from each box onto plates in front of Ruby and Maude. She kept the small container of vegetable fried rice for herself.

"See, Ruby knows how to use chopsticks," Opal said appreciatively.

"I'm about to use some chopsticks," Maude muttered. "To stab you with."

"All that inner rage," Opal said sadly. "Too much caffeine and not enough fiber in your diet, I'd say. Anyway, hurry up and let's get on with shopping. I figured you and Ruby would have bought half the town by now."

"Ruby was trying to, but then we started looking for you," Maude explained. "We've spent the last hour or more fighting through the crowds trying to find you."

"Why in the world were you looking for me?" Opal asked. "I wasn't lost."

"Because we didn't know where you were, Opal," Ruby said. "But anyway, we're all together now. This food is delicious by the way. What is it?"

"Mongolian Beef. Min told me they use a special recipe," Opal said.

Maude eyed her wearily before studying the food in front of her.

"Eat up, Maude. Min says it's the best!" Opal said.

"I don't trust you," Maude told her.

"Don't be rude!" Ruby whispered. "You have to try new things. When in Rome," she shrugged.

"We ain't in Rome," Maude said. "We already went there once!"

"Maude, you really should see someone about all these unresolved issues you have. It's not good to let things build up," Opal suggested. "Here, try this tonic I got." She pulled a tiny vial from her purse and sprinkled the contents over Maude's plate.

"I don't have unresolved issues. I have issues with you trying to kill me every time you feed me something new," Maude said. "What are you doing?"

"It's medicinal," Opal explained.

"I've seen your type of medicinal mumbo jumbo before," Maude said. "No way!"

"Oh hush, it's powdered rhino's horn. It's great for arthritis and gout. Have you seen your feet?"

"Powdered what? What's wrong with you?" Maude asked in an outrage.

"The list of historical uses also include headaches, hallucinations, high blood pressure, typhoid, snakebite, food poisoning, and even possession by spirits," Opal continued. "All things that you probably suffer from. There's no need to suffer any longer. We can help you."

"Help me right over a cliff," Maude muttered. "Y'all hurry up and eat. Then I'm going to find me a hotdog cart when we get back to the hotel."

"Now Maude, there's no reason to bring that up," Ruby tried to calm the situation.

"What?" Opal asked innocently.

"That time you pushed me over a cliff and tried to drown me!" Maude said.

"You're always exaggerating things," Opal said. "Besides, that's what friends are for."

Before Maude could launch into another tirade, Ruby jumped in. "Are y'all ready to do some serious shopping? I found lots of bargains out there."

"Absolutely! Min told me where to get the best things," Opal said. "Come on, y'all."

Maude stared at Opal open mouthed.

"We're always waiting on her, bless her heart," Opal told Ruby. "Honestly, we really should get her a collar or something that can track her whereabouts. She's always getting lost."

~⌐Chapter Nine⌐~

Later the next morning, Ruby tried on three different outfits before she was content with the pink sweater that felt warm.

"What purse goes best with this sweater?" Ruby asked. She spread out her seven new purses that she had bought during their shopping excursion the night before. "I think this blue one is so cute. I'm thinking I'm going to carry this salmon one though. It's fancier than what I normally carry, but I think that's ok. I want to blend in. Here Maude, you can carry this black one if you'd like."

"I think I'll stick with the one I brought," Maude said. "I still don't know why you bought all those. You know you won't ever have the time to use them all. You can only carry one purse at a time."

"Ruby can carry as many purses as she wants," Opal shrugged. "She can be the new bag lady of Rhinestone. We'll find her a nice little park bench and everything."

Ruby playfully tossed one of the smaller bags at Opal who caught it easily. The three friends finished getting ready and made their way down to the lobby. They had slept in pretty late after an intense evening of shopping. On the way back to their hotel the night before, Maude made them stop at a donut shop that was open round the clock. They had ended up staying up late playing cards thanks to that surge of sugar. Now that it was nearing lunchtime, they were all pretty hungry.

True to form, Opal had found out the name of an authentic Italian restaurant during one of her many conversations with anyone who happened to be standing near her. They walked in and were greeted with the most amazing aromas. Freshly made noodles and breads of all kinds were drying behind the counter.

"This place looks heavenly," Ruby gushed. "Look at those beautiful paintings!"

"Smells delicious!" Maude said.

"My sources never disappoint!" Opal smiled.

They were seated in a booth near the back of the restaurant and greeted by a charming waiter named Antonio. He flirted with them a bit and raved about their accents.

"He reminds me of that nice young man we met in Italy. You remember when we stayed at that hostel in Rome?" Ruby asked.

"Niccolo," Opal smiled. "I still remember our late night vespa ride together."

"There is something about Italian men," Ruby blushed.

"Ruby!" Maude said. "You can't say things like that. You're a happily married woman!"

Ruby laughed. "Yes, I am, but it doesn't hurt to admire nice people. The good Lord creates masterpieces all around."

They were laughing loudly when Antonio came back with their drinks. It took a few minutes to decide what to order. Everything on the menu looked so delicious. They decided to each get a different dish and try a sampling of items. Ruby ordered the fettuccine, Opal tried the eggplant lasagna, and Maude asked for the sampler platter with chicken marsala, pasta carbonara, and stuffed shells.

"What?" Maude asked Opal who was staring at her.

"Do you think you've ordered enough?" Opal asked.

"I got enough to share," Maude shrugged. "Besides, you didn't let me finish my Chinese food last night. I'm starving. They're bringing those free little plates of bread, right?"

Ruby knew the conversation was heading for trouble. "So, what would you like to do today?" She asked, quickly changing the subject.

They spent the next twenty minutes chatting about possible adventures for the day ahead. When Antonio brought out the entrees, they spent a few more moments quietly admiring their waiter before digging into their food.

"That is one good looking hunk of man," Maude said.

"You're old enough to be his grandmother," Opal added.

"So am I," Ruby laughed. "And so are you for that matter."

They were all laughing hysterically when Antonio came back around to check on them and refill their drinks. Maude and Ruby had each tried portions of every dish on the table before calling it quits.

Maude stretched loudly and yawned. "I think I'm going to visit the restroom before we head out sightseeing," she told them. She stood up and walked back toward the kitchens. Ruby watched her go while Opal paid the bill.

"Ready to go?" Opal asked once she signed her name on the receipt.

Ruby nodded and stood up to gather her purse. "Wait a minute, is that who I think it is?" Ruby gulped.

Opal turned around in her chair and peered over the divider. "Oh boy! This ought to be good."

"I don't want to be rude, but maybe if we duck down a little bit, maybe she won't see us," Ruby whispered. "I don't want to upset Maude so early on in the trip."

But Opal had other plans. She popped out of her chair and scrambled over to where Nadine had been seated. "Hey Nadine," she called. "It's Opal and Ruby! What a small world."

Nadine gasped and dropped her fork on the floor. "What are you two doing here?"

"Same as you," beamed Opal. "How was your flight?"

"Not bad. Only one small delay in Washington D.C. yesterday afternoon," smiled Nadine. "Wait a minute, aren't you missing your stooge?"

"Nadine, that wasn't kind," Ruby admonished.

"I'm sorry, Ruby. You're right. But where is Maude?" Nadine asked.

"She's in the restroom. And we were just leaving. Enjoy your meal," Ruby smiled. "It was good to see you."

"Have you seen much of the sights yet?" Nadine asked. "By the time I landed yesterday, I was too tired to do much. I saw a delightful little concert in the park across the street though."

"Oh, that sounds nice. Where are you staying?" Opal asked, ignoring Ruby's insistence.

"At the loveliest place," Nadine crooned. "You may have heard of it, the Plaza."

"Oh my," Ruby gasped.

"Martin did such a fabulous job with this trip," Nadine continued. "Where are you staying?"

"Make sure you take the ferry over to the Statue of Liberty," Ruby added, ignoring Nadine's question.

"Gorgeous views. Oh, well, we must be going. Have a great stay, Nadine!"

Ruby yanked Opal by the arm and drug her towards the door. "Hopefully, Maude won't see her over yonder in the corner. I swear, Martin Rhodes is a mess," Ruby scowled. She stopped right outside the door and turned to Opal. "We don't breathe a word of this to Maude," she instructed. "We don't mention Nadine or anything of the sort."

"Yes ma'am," Opal saluted with a smile.

"What are y'all going on about?" Maude asked behind them.

"Ahh! You scared me," Ruby gasped. "Are you ok?"

"Of course I'm okay. I just went to the bathroom I'm fine. Are you ok?" Maude asked.

"Great," Ruby breathed a sigh of relief. "What's next on the itinerary?"

"Are you sure you're ok, Ruby?" Maude asked again. "You look like you either ate something bad or saw a ghost."

"She's just so overtaken with emotion at being in the Big Apple," Opal clarified.

"I feel the same way!" Maude agreed. "Let's walk up this way and see about that giant toy store Mavis told us about. We need to find her and Wilbur some great gifts. Nothing says New York City like a big doll or teddy bear."

"Great idea," nodded Ruby. "I already got them both shirts from the park, too." She looked over her shoulder at the doors of the restaurant and breathed a sigh of relief. Nadine was too busy eating her salad to notice Maude leaving the restaurant. It was best to keep those two separated as long as possible. Imagine running into each other in a city as large as New York.

"Let's go!" Ruby tucked her arm into Maude's elbow and practically dragged her along.

"Good gracious, Ruby!" Maude almost jogged to keep up with Ruby's sudden burst of enthusiasm. "What has gotten into you?"

"You know how much Ruby loves to shop!" Opal beamed as she jogged past them.

"Will y'all stop! I'm too fat to run!" Maude laughed while she and Ruby caught up with Opal who had stopped a few yards away. They were well out of sight of the restaurant now.

"Why are y'all trying to kill me?" Maude asked, clutching a stitch in her side.

"All part of the adventure, Maude. We're trying to keep you from getting any older," Opal said.

"By giving me a heart attack?" Maude tried to take a deep breath.

Ruby laughed, but she too was glad for the chance to stop their quick little jog. "Sorry Maude. I guess I got carried away. Let's just walk the rest of the way."

"About time you came to your senses," Maude said, but there was a smile across her face. It was great watching Ruby being silly every now and again.

They took off down Fifth Avenue and marveled at the high-rise buildings that loomed above them. They didn't make them this big in Rhinestone, or anywhere in the nearby counties. The toy store was even more magnificent than any of them could have imagined. After watching the blockbuster film that had highlighted FAO Schwarz the year before, they thought they had known what to expect, but being in the middle of the giant store with life-size toys was overwhelming. Stuffed animals, puzzles, books, and electronic devices adorned the walls and shelves all around them. Two hours later, they all walked out of the front doors loaded down with shopping bags and wrapped packages.

"How in the world are we going to get this back to Rhinestone?" Maude asked.

"We'll worry about that later," Opal chirped. She hailed a taxi and together they all stuffed their newfound treasures into the trunk and piled inside. After unloading their bags at their room at the hotel, they scrambled back down to the lobby and jumped into the back of another cab to find a nice place to relax for the evening.

"You know what I'd really like to do?" Maude asked.

"What?" Ruby asked.

"I'd love to go to a real-life speakeasy. You know, one of those like the 1920s," Maude said, staring out the window.

"Speakeasy?" the driver asked. "I know just the place. Hold on!"

They stopped at an inconspicuous metal gate that read "The Lower East Side Toy Company."

"What is this place?" Ruby asked.

"Speakeasy you wanted to go to," the driver grunted.

"I don't see anything that looks like a bar," Ruby mumbled.

"It's kinda hidden. Go through the gate and through the alleyway. You'll see some stairs. The Back Room is the best joint in town," the driver assured them.

Maude and Ruby glanced at each other. They had a sneaking suspicion that he might be setting them up for something.

"Trust me," the driver said.

That didn't settle their nerves. Before they could tell the driver they had changed their minds, Opal had opened her door and jumped out in the evening breeze.

"Well, when in Rome," they heard her say as she opened the gate and disappeared from view.

"We better go after her," Maude said. She handed the driver some cash and they darted after their friend. "Opal, wait for us!"

They found Opal waiting for them in an alleyway. "I don't feel comfortable," Ruby began, but Maude cut her off. "Let's go!" she said exuberantly.

They slowly climbed up a set of stairs and found a dimly lit den fitted with a shimmering bar.

"Oh, this is beautiful," Ruby whispered.

They had stepped back in time. In the center of the room hung a large chandelier. The fireplace beneath it provided warmth to the patrons sitting on the sofas. There was oak paneling throughout. It looked like they had walked onto to movie set.

"Oooh, will you look at this place," Opal beamed. "I bet they have a secret passage somewhere."

"Opal, don't you dare!" Maude warned her.

"What?" Opal asked innocently. "Wouldn't you like to find a secret passageway sometime. That's on my bucket list."

"Be that as it may, we are not trying to find a secret passageway in here," Maude told her.

"Look at those tea cups! I wonder if they're for sale!" Ruby wondered aloud.

Opal waltzed away to the counter while Maude and Ruby sat down at a small table.

"Bottled beer is put in these cute little brown bags," Opal gushed. She handed Maude a brown bag and sat down next to Ruby.

"Why?" Ruby asked. "Is it illegal?"

"No, it's just cool," Opal explained. "The bartender said this place was actually a speakeasy from the prohibition era. That's the way they did it back then. Go ahead Maude, try your contraband. I got a cute little cocktail for myself."

"I want a pretty teacup, too," Ruby said.

"You don't drink, Ruby," Opal said. "But you can hold my teacup if you want."

Maude finished her beer quickly and walked to the bar for another. When she finished that one, she asked Opal what the best cocktail that represented the 1920s would be.

"Don't you worry, Maude. I've got you!" Opal grinned. She jumped up and all but sprinted to the counter. When she returned, she was carrying three teacups and set them down in front of Maude.

"All of those?" Ruby gasped.

"I'm sure they're watered down," Opal winked.

Maude wasted no time in downing the three teacups. "Is that all? I guess folks in the 1920s didn't hold their liquor like I can." She burped loudly and shook her head. "Is it bright in here to yall? I think someone turned the lights on after we got in here. And it's getting warm. Help me get out of this sweater."

Opal tugged on one sleeve while Ruby helped Maude pull the gray sweater over her head. "Why don't you sit down for a bit," Ruby suggested.

"I'm going to lay down right here," Maude yawned. She balled up her sweater and plopped down on the bench. Within seconds, she was sound asleep. Opal and Ruby launched into a conversation about the time they held a yard sale on Main Street. Maude's snores began to bother other patrons. Ruby was getting embarrassed by their furtive looks and whispers.

"It's better when she sleeps," Opal called out. "At least she didn't run off to get another tattoo this time," Opal said. "The last time she got this tipsy, she came back with more than she bargained for." She laughed hard at her comment, even though the patrons at the nearby tables didn't seem to get her joke.

"Shh," Ruby hissed. "Don't tell Maude's business to a stranger. They don't need to know that Maude has a value brand Rolling Stones tattoo on her rear end."

"She could get another one of the other cheek. You know, to balance her out," Opal offered.

"I don't think it's appropriate to be having this kind of conversation in public," Ruby blushed.

"Suit yourself," Opal smiled. She tipped the remainder of the liquid into her mouth and gathered up the teacups on the table to return to the counter. "You wake up the sleeping bear and I'll clean up our mess."

Ruby nudged Maude who grunted loudly in return. The other patrons stared at them. Some of them began to laugh when Maude warned Ruby to watch out for the aliens.

"I don't know what you gave her, but she's had enough," Ruby told Opal sternly

"She never could hold her liquor," Opal shook her head. "I asked the bartender to call us a cab. It'll probably be outside by the time we drag her out there."

⌒Chapter Ten⌒

"Up you go, Maude. Just a few more steps," Opal yelled loudly.

"I'm not deaf!" Maude croaked back.

"Shh, y'all quit," Ruby hissed. She held Maude's purse as she watched Maude stagger through the front doors of the Plaza. "Let's just get to the elevators and get her in the shower. Goodness gracious, Maude, you are too old to be acting this way."

"Pish posh," muttered Maude. She leaned against the wall near the elevators and waited for the doors to open. While she waited, she sang an offkey rendition of Deck the Halls in a rough British accent.

"Deck the hall with boughs of trollies. I don't know the rest, but it sounds like a mess," Maude sang.

"I don't think that's how it goes," Opal interrupted.

"Never mind that," Ruby said. "We've got to get her upstairs and into the room. People are starting to stare."

Opal turned and began waving at a few of the onlookers. "Hi there," she winked.

Ruby wanted to find somewhere to crawl and hide.

"See, Ruby, they're looking at me. I always draw a crowd wherever I go," Opal continued to smile around the room.

"We're never going to be able to show our faces again," Ruby mumbled, shaking her head. "We're going to be banned from New York City. They're never going to let us back up here to visit."

"Don't be silly, Ruby. They can't ban us from an entire city. I mean, they could ban us from the hotel for sure, but not the entire city," Opal tried to reassure her.

"Oh my goodness," Ruby shook her head.

"And we've seen Maude in worse shape," Opal continued. "Really, this is pretty mild for her."

"Thank the Lord for that," Ruby said.

The elevators opened and Ruby pushed Maude inside. Opal twirled herself in the elevator and bumped into the back of a woman wearing a bright red dress, a long fur coat, sunglasses, and a mink hat.

"Oh, excuse me, ma'am," Opal smiled. "Nadine?"

"Opal?" Nadine exclaimed. "What are you doing here?"

"Madine? Did you say Madine? Maude slurred before she turned on a dime and faced the woman in red. "You've got to be kidding me."

"Maude! There you are. What is that smell?" Nadine turned up her nose and coughed into her shawl.

"I'm taking the stairs," Maude sputtered. Before Ruby could pull her back, she burst through the elevator doors with a sudden burst of energetic sobriety and left Opal, Ruby, and Nadine staring after her.

"She can't manage the stairs on her own!" Ruby exclaimed. It was too late to go after her. The doors closed and they were traveling skyward.

Opal shrugged and turned back to Nadine who was still staring awkwardly at the doors. "So, what floor are you on?"

"Twelfth floor," Nadine replied. She took off her sunglasses and tucked them into her matching handbag. "And you?"

Opal began to laugh and looked at Ruby. "This is hilarious," she cackled.

The elevator door dinged and opened wide. Nadine stepped out and waved her hand dismissively. She seemed to have embraced the glamour of the Big Apple wholeheartedly. "I hope you have a good night. And hopefully Maude, um, feels better soon."

Opal and Ruby scurried out of the elevator before the doors closed on them. "As fate would have it, we're on the same floor," Opal smiled. "Goodnight Nadine! Sleep tight, don't let the bed bugs bite."

Nadine dropped her handbag on the floor and rolled her eyes. "Of course y'all are." She picked up her handbag and walked down the hallway.

"We've got to find Maude," Ruby said exasperatedly.

"Hold on a second. Let's see which room she goes into," Opal paused. They watched as Nadine stopped three doors away from their room.

"Oh dear Lord. Maude is going to have a fit when she finds out that we're neighbors," Ruby shook her head. "Let's go find her and make sure she isn't stuck between floors somewhere."

"Well, you wanted an adventure," Opal sang happily.

"Not that much of an adventure," Ruby pushed the down button on the elevator. "It's more like the New York edition of the Rhinestone Circus."

They stepped back onto the elevator without looking at the gentleman standing there.

"Main lobby, please," Ruby motioned at the panel of numbers.

"Sure thing," he answered, pushing the button she requested.

Ruby looked up immediately. "Thank you," she said. Ruby didn't trust herself to speak for the next few minutes. She kept stealing sideways glances at the handsome man sharing the elevator with them.

He got off at the third floor and wished them a good night. "Oh my goodness, Opal. Do you know who that was?" Ruby gushed.

"Who?" Opal asked.

"It was Michael Douglas!" Ruby squealed.

Opal sighed heavily. "Ruby, did you have some of Maude's drink?"

"Of course not!" Ruby said.

Opal patted her arm sympathetically. "That wasn't Michael Douglas."

"I'm sure of it," Ruby told her. "I'd know that voice anywhere. And that thick hair with that cleft chin. He's as handsome as his father was. I'm certain that was him."

"Okay," Opal rolled her eyes. "If you say so."

"It was him, Opal Tyler," Ruby was firm.

"I'm sure it was," Opal nodded slowly.

"You stop that," Ruby stepped off the elevator. "I'm positive it was him."

Opal was still nodding. "And Maude might have made it all the way up twelve flights of stairs by now. Or she could have stopped off by his room for a nightcap. It's really anyone's guess what could happen tonight."

Ruby turned to her. "You just hush. Let's go find Maude." Ruby marched off toward the stairs muttering about how she would recognize Michael Douglas anywhere. Several guests turned in her direction, but said nothing to her.

Opal shrugged and followed Ruby to the stairs. The emergency exit stairs were in sharp contrast to the rest of the building. Whereas the lobby displayed the height of elegance, the stairwell was little more than a barren concrete staircase that wove its way to the very top of the building.

"Maude, hello? Ground control to Maude Cooper!" Opal howled. Her voice echoed through the floors below.

"Shh! Stop that," Ruby ordered. "Let's just look instead of waking up the whole building."

"Ruby, unless she's hanging over the side, we're not going to be able to see her," Opal said.

"Well, she couldn't have gotten far," Ruby said.

Opal shrugged and took the first couple of steps in her usual stride.

"Opal, wait. Do you hear that?" Ruby asked.

They both listened for a moment to the faint humming coming from above them. Then suddenly, the unmistakable caterwauling that could only be Maude's singing.

"Start spreadin' da hues, we're leavin' today," Maude bellowed. "New Pork, New Pork!"

"Well, her lyrics are getting closer at least," Opal smiled.

"Oh my word," Ruby stammered. "Let's go find her and get her up to the room."

They rushed up the stairs to find Maude sitting on the first step beside the door leading to the third floor, happily humming away at her makeshift tune.

"Thank goodness she didn't make it any further. Let's get her to the elevator," Ruby said. She grabbed Maude by the elbow.

"I'm tired," Maude shook her head. "I think I'll take a wee nap right here." She leaned her head against the wall.

"Maude, you can't sleep here. We've got to get you upstairs," Ruby pleaded.

Opal took a slightly different approach. She braced herself with one foot on the step above Maude, reached underneath Maude's shoulder, and hoisted her friend up from where she sat.

"Watch out, Opal. You almost knocked me down," Ruby told her after catching her suddenly upright friend awkwardly.

"Sorry Rubes! Been working out. Guess I don't know my own strength," Opal smiled.

"I told ya, I don't wanna dance," Maude said as she tried to focus on Opal's face.

"We're going to take you someplace where you can have a nice long nap," Opal assured her.

They each draped one of Maude's arms over their shoulders and half carried her out of the stairwell back to the elevator. Fifteen minutes later, Maude was happily snoring away on her bed.

"I thought you wanted to get her in the shower," Opal said, wiping some sweat from her brow.

Ruby stood fanning herself. "She can take care of that in the morning. I'm exhausted. I'm too old to be carrying her home from a bender."

"She never could hold her liquor," Opal said.

"Then why in the world did you give her something so strong," Ruby asked.

Opal shrugged. "She said she wanted to experience a real speakeasy. Who am I to deny her dream?"

Ruby shook her head and headed to the bathroom to get ready for bed.

By mid-morning the next day, Maude rolled over and held a pillow over her face. She grumbled incoherently and curled up into the fetal position. "What in the world was in those drinks last night?" Maude moaned. Ruby handed her a bundle of ice wrapped in a wash cloth for her to hold against her forehead.

"Nothing too strong. I told them you'd like a little hanky panky in the sidecar. They said it was the bee's knees," Opal winked at her.

Maude stared at her out of one eye since it was the only one that seemed to want to focus at the moment. "What in the world are you going on about?" she mumbled.

"The drinks I ordered for you. I got you some classics. A hanky panky, a sidecar, and the bee's knees," Opal stood up and began her morning stretches.

"I'm sure those are just colorful names," Ruby told her. "I'm sure she didn't tell them you wanted anything else." Ruby shot Opal a serious look.

"I wouldn't put anything past her," Maude closed her eyes.

By the time Opal and Ruby had finished getting ready, Maude felt almost human enough to jump in the shower. They were sitting on the beds sorting through the packages Ruby had bought when Maude finally stepped out of the bathroom.

"Well it's about time. I was about to come in there and make sure you didn't drown," Opal said.

"I think I'm okay now," Maude said. "As long as it's not too bright."

"I'll tell the sun to hold it down a bit," Opal reassured her. "Come on. Let's get something to eat."

"Nothing too heavy," Maude muttered. She occasionally held onto the wall for extra support.

Ruby and Opal both looked at her.

"What was in those drinks last night?" Ruby whispered to Opal.

Opal shrugged. "Nothing some fresh air won't cure."

They stepped out into the hallway and turned toward the elevator. Ruby eyed the rooms they passed wearily. Hopefully, Nadine was already out and about seeing all the sights New York had to offer. They were getting a later start than they had wanted after all. It was entirely possible that Nadine was not even in her room as they passed by the door. Even still, Ruby kept a close eye on the door silently willing it to remain shut. She didn't think she could handle their full-fledged war of attrition right here on the twelfth floor of the Plaza.

"You know, I had the strangest dream last night," Maude began.

Ruby turned quickly to Opal. "What was that?" she asked Maude.

"I dreamed that Nadine was staying here and we saw her," Maude rubbed her head. "Even in my dream she was just as ornery as always."

"You don't say," Opal began, but Ruby elbowed her before she could say anything else. "Ouch!"

"Don't you dare," Ruby warned her in a hushed whisper.

"She's bound to see her," Opal said. "We're three doors down."

"Hush," Ruby told her through gritted teeth.

Maude was ambling several steps behind them trying to shield her eyes from the light created by the sconces along the wall. "Let's stop by the gift shop and pick up some aspirin," she told them once she had caught up to them at the elevator. "And maybe some Alka Seltzer." She put her hand on her stomach.

"Alright," Ruby agreed, eyeing Opal closely in case she decided to give Maude more information about Nadine.

"I still don't understand why you don't want to tell Maude that Nadine is staying three doors down from us," Opal told Ruby as they waited in the lobby for Maude to return with her medicine.

"Oh, you know how Maude gets. Her feud with Nadine has been going on for decades," Ruby said.

"Better to tell her now though," Opal nodded. "She can't yell as loud with a hangover."

Ruby stared at her in disbelief.

"It's true," Opal shrugged.

They looked up to see Maude walking toward them. "Let's find a place to sit down and eat so I can wash this stuff down," she said, holding up the bag of hangover cures she had just purchased.

"We could grab a bite to eat at the restaurant here if you like," Ruby offered. She pointed in the direction of the restaurant.

"Sure, that's fine by me," Maude agreed.

They all turned to walk over to the cafe located on the other side of the lobby when the doors of the elevator opened up and Nadine stepped out. She was dressed like a movie star with oversized sunglasses and a chiffon scarf.

"Eggplant is not her color," Opal mumbled. "Doesn't do a thing for her complexion."

"Huh?" Maude turned to Opal. "What are you talking about?

Ruby looked up and almost tripped over her own two feet, but Maude caught her.

"You sure you're not the one with the hangover?" Maude asked Ruby.

"On second thought, there's a little diner around the corner we haven't tried yet," Ruby said, quickly changing her mind. Ruby grabbed Maude's arm at the elbow and swung her around before Maude could recognize her nemesis.

"What in the world has gotten into you, Ruby?" Maude asked. "I thought you wanted to eat here."

Ruby was now dragging Maude out of the main entrance. "I think Opal might be right. I think you need some sunshine and fresh air."

"Now don't go crazy and start acting like Opal!" Maude fumed. "I can't handle both of y'all crazy. I need somebody on my side." Maude struggled to release Ruby's grip from her arm.

"Crazy am I?" Opal asked. "Well, at least I'm not the one who's been in a fight with my neighbor forever and a day."

"Nadine deserves it," Maude began.

"Y'all two stop it!" Ruby told them. "Let's go to the diner and have a nice relaxing breakfast. Maude can take her medicine while we eat. Then we can go see the Empire State Building."

"I thought we were going to see the World Trade Center," Maude said.

"We can do that, too," Ruby agreed. "As long as you can handle the cab ride over there."

"I'll be fine," Maude assured her. "You know food fixes everything."

∽Chapter Eleven∽

"So what first? The Empire State Building or the World Trade Center?" Ruby asked after they had each had their fill of bacon and pancakes.

Maude turned to guidebook in every direction. "This thing says the Empire State Building is closer, but I can't tell which direction the darn thing is. All these buildings look the same. At least in Rhinestone we use more color in our paints."

"It's this way," Opal pointed to the right. "But we better take a cab. Maude isn't as young as we are, Ruby. She might give out before we get there." She winked in Maude's direction and took off.

"One of these days, Opal Tyler," Maude huffed, but Opal had already skipped over the curb and flagged down a taxi.

"No use arguing with her," Ruby told Maude with a smile. "I might give out before we walk there, too. This could turn out to be another full day of hair-raising adventures!"

"One of these days we will be too old for all this drama," Maude added.

"But not today," Opal laughed. She held the door for Maude and Ruby and then climbed into the backseat with them.

"Aren't we a little crowded back here?" Maude yelped. "I thought you were going to sit up front. If you aren't, let me out and I will."

"Just a cozy little Maude sandwich in the back," Opal sang, and shifted closer to Maude to wedge her tightly between her and Ruby.

"Is that Rockefeller Center?" Ruby asked, leaning over Maude to get a better look. "I've always wanted to see that at Christmas time."

Maude pushed Ruby back into her seat and closed her eyes. After last night's adventures, she didn't trust herself to look at the scenery rushing by.

"We should come back up and see it in December," Opal said. "I'll add it to the bucket list when I get home."

They continued on Fifth Avenue until the driver suddenly turned and zipped into a stop in front of the largest building Ruby had ever seen.

"Here ya go," the driver said.

Ruby and Maude stood on the sidewalk looking up with wonder at one of the most famous feats of modern architecture.

"It's hard to believe King Kong actually climbed that thing, isn't it?" Opal said as she joined them on the sidewalk.

Maude opened her mouth to say something, but was stopped by Ruby stomping on her foot. "Ow," she said to Ruby.

Ruby shook her head and followed Opal into the lobby.

"It's like stepping back in time," Ruby said.

"It certainly is crowded in here," Maude said.

"What are they all standing around for?" Ruby asked.

"Another gift shop probably," Maude replied. "And before you even think about it, no! I ain't carrying all the bags anymore. We're already going to have to rent a whole plane to stuff your souvenirs on board."

"Y'all quit squabbling and follow me. Come on. I know a shortcut," Opal said. She led them around a corner through another corridor that opened to the stairs.

"You can't be serious," Maude said. She had stopped and looked up. "They make you take the stairs in this thing?"

"Well, maybe they didn't actually have elevators back when it was built," Ruby offered diplomatically.

"Elevators have been around forever, Ruby," Maude grumbled and rolled her eyes. "It better be worth all this."

"The view is unbelievable!" Opal added, leading the way.

"How would she know?" Maude inquired.

"I've seen all the movies," Opal reminded her. "If you didn't fall asleep ten minutes into each film, you could, too."

"Come on, Maude. When in Rome after all," Ruby said, following Opal up the stairs.

"I seem to remember she got me in trouble then, too," Maude grumbled.

"How many stories is this thing?" Maude huffed. She had to pause to catch her breath before she could take another step. "What is it, like eighty?"

"One hundred and two," Opal called down from above. "We should be close now. Keep it moving. One foot in front of the other."

"You said that twenty minutes ago," Maude yelled from the stairs below Opal. Ruby was somewhere between the two with a pained expression on her face.

"And now we're twenty minutes closer than we were," Opal said.

"It hasn't been twenty minutes," Ruby said, looking down at her watch." Come on, Maude. We can make it," she encouraged.

"She's only doing this so I'll be too tired to kill her later," Maude grumbled as she caught up with Ruby. "I could always pawn it off on account of her trying to kill me with exercise."

"What do you want to kill her for this time?" Ruby asked.

"I don't know, but I'm sure I'll think of something," Maude said. She took a deep breath before grabbing onto the rail and hoisting herself forward.

Ten minutes later, they stepped out onto the observation deck.

Opal had not been wrong, the view was spectacular. They could see perfectly in every direction for miles and miles. It was a clear morning, which gave them an eagle's eye view of New York City.

"That gentleman over there says we can see six states from here," Ruby said in awe. "New Jersey, Pennsylvania, Connecticut, Massachusetts, and Delaware."

"That's only five states, Ruby," Maude corrected.

"Well, New York is the other state," Ruby said gently. "I didn't think I'd have to include that one in the summary since we're here."

"Oh, right. I knew that," Maude huffed. "I won't be able to see anything until I can breathe again anyway,"

"And this is where Cary Grant was going to meet Deborah Kerr, but she stood him up," Opal said.

"What are you talking about?" Maude asked.

"An Affair to Remember," Opal said. "Honestly, Maude, you really need to keep up with popular culture more. So many movies are set right here on top of this very building but it looks so much bigger in real life."

"Would you like to know more?" the man Ruby had mentioned earlier suddenly said behind them.

"Yes, please," Ruby smiled.

"You can see Rockefeller Plaza Center, the Chrysler Building, the World Trade Center, Central Park, Times Square, the Statue of Liberty, Union Square, and so much more," the man said. "You really can't beat the views here. And of course, the architecture is one of a kind. It was a phenomenal feat of achievement."

"It's just like I always imagined," Ruby said. "Just magical."

"Absolutely," he agreed. "Do you have any questions?"

"Not a question, but more of a concern. You'd think they could have put in an elevator at some point," Maude said.

The man looked at her as if she had two heads. "We have elevators. They're right over there."

"You mean, we didn't have to climb the stairs?" Maude asked.

"That's certainly an option, but most people don't really want to climb all those stories. Most of our visitors don't take the stairs," he said.

Maude looked at Ruby. "I knew I was going to have a reason to kill her."

"Now Maude, she never said there wasn't an elevator," Ruby said.

"She tricked me into taking the stairs," Maude huffed.

"She just wanted you to get your exercise," Ruby laughed. "And you didn't want to wait in that line."

"I would have waited an hour if it meant I didn't have to literally climb the Empire State Building!" Maude shrieked.

"Oh hush, you're making another scene. I'm surprised they haven't put your picture up on the bridges yet warning people about your temper!" Ruby admonished.

"They haven't seen my temper in full form yet. I've been on my best behavior," Maude said proudly.

Ruby decided not to reply. She looked around quickly. "Where's Opal?"

Maude shrugged and looked around for one last breathtaking look. "How do we get to the World Trade Center from here?" she asked the man.

"The easiest way is to take Fifth to Broadway and follow it down. That way is probably pretty thick right now. Your best bet might be to head over to FDR and follow it around past the Battery," the man explained. "That might be a little dangerous, but you look like you can handle yourself."

"Thanks," Maude said. Ruby had spotted Opal across the deck.

"Come on crazy, we have directions and this time, I'm in charge," Maude said. She drug Opal away from a man half her age who was pointing at different sights through the coin operated binoculars.

"Adeus Mateo," Opal grinned. "I hope you find your lucky penny."

"Lucky penny?" Ruby asked.

"I don't know," Opal shrugged. "Some things might have been lost in translation. I don't speak Portuguese all that well."

"The fact that you speak it at all astounds me," Ruby chuckled.

"And this time we're taking the elevator!" Maude said.

Opal shrugged. "I figured you would have wanted to take it on the way up."

Before Maude could turn around and comment the doors opened and Ruby pushed Maude inside. They made it down to the lobby a couple of minutes later.

They stepped out onto the crowded street.

"Which way?" Ruby asked Maude.

"Come on," Maude said. She stepped over to the corner and flagged down a taxi. When they were settled in, she turned to the driver. "We need to take Broadway over to FDR and Fifth past the Battering."

The driver turned around and looked at her. "You need to go where?" he asked.

"We're taking FDR and Fifth over to Broadway past the Batting," Maude tried again.

"That's not even a thing," Opal said.

"Where exactly are you trying to go?" the driver asked.

"The World Trade Center," Ruby said.

"That's how the guy upstairs told us to get there," Maude said defensively.

"Did he say take FDR to the Battery?" the driver asked again.

"That sounds right," Maude said. "Close enough."

The driver shook his head. He'd never heard it called the Batting or the Battering before. Tourists certainly had a way of coming up with interesting names for the landmarks in his hometown.

"World Trade Center. Got it," he said. He pulled out into traffic and set off down the street.

It took almost an hour to get there. A pipe had burst along the way and cars were being rerouted around the confusion. When they finally arrived, Maude, Opal, and Ruby stepped out of the taxi and looked around at the giant office center.

"So, what is the big hype about this place again?" Maude asked.

"Some of the tallest buildings in the world," Opal explained. "Used to be the tallest, but you know how men are. Always in some sort of competition with one another to have the biggest toy."

"I don't think office buildings are considered toys," Ruby interrupted.

"I speak in metaphors," Opal smiled.

"Office buildings?" Maude said. "I think we can cross this off the bucket list."

"Don't you want to go up?" Ruby asked.

"Not really," Maude shrugged. "Is it the same view that we just had? Because I see a donut cart across the way and I'd like to see what views they can offer."

"Oh, alright," mumbled Ruby. "Come on Opal, Maude has decided she can't possibly take another step without a greasy donut."

"I'll meet you all over there directly," Opal said. "I'm here now and I'm going to make the trek to the top. I just feel like I maybe won't have another chance. Why don't you join me?"

"Thanks Opal, but I guess I better stay out here with Maude. My feet are pretty sore anyway. But take the camera and get some good pictures," Ruby added.

"Yes ma'am," Opal saluted. She turned and joined the line headed to the top of one of the Twin Towers.

"These donuts better be worth it," Ruby sighed. She hurried down the way to where Maude was already ordering at a vendor's cart.

Maude took the box of donuts from the man and opened the box with gusto. "Smell these, Ruby. Better take one quickly before I eat them all myself. This is my lunch after all."

Ruby took one of the donuts and bit into it. It was indeed delicious, but she didn't think she could eat an entire box full. "Save some room. Remember that Opal is taking us to that dinner theater show tonight. She's really excited about it."

"But that's not for another few hours. I need to keep my energy up," Maude swallowed another donut and shook the powdered sugar off of her fingers.

They sat down on a bench between the two towers and watched the people rushing by.

"Everyone certainly seems to be in a hurry," Ruby remarked.

"Sure is different from Rhinestone, isn't it?" Maude agreed.

"It's a completely different world up here," Ruby said. "I love our visit, but I don't think I could live here."

"Yeah, it is different," Maude took another bite of the donut. "I'm really glad we got to take this trip. And it's not over yet!"

"I know you've been excited about it for a while now. Is it everything you thought it would be?" Ruby asked.

Maude nodded. "And a bit more. It's hard to imagine this many people in one place."

"And these buildings," Ruby added. "We don't have a hundred buildings in Rhinestone and they have hundreds of buildings with that many floors. It's really incredible."

"It would be nice to come back and see Rockefeller Center all decorated up at Christmas time," Maude said. "I bet that is beautiful."

"Opal said she was adding it to the bucket list," Ruby said.

Maude shook her head. "I think Opal's bucket list is about five miles long now. She's never met an adventure she didn't want to take."

"She certainly likes to keep things interesting," Ruby smiled.

"That she does," Maude nodded.

"What would we do without her?" Ruby asked.

Maude sat quietly.

Ruby looked at her. "You okay?"

"Yeah, I'm just thinking," Maude said.

"About what?" Ruby said.

"About how peaceful life would be without Opal," Maude smiled with a wink.

"Oh stop that!" Ruby laughed. "We both know you'd be completely lost without her. We both would. Life would be boring without her."

"You're probably right," Maude nodded. "Guess we're stuck with her now."

"You have to admit, we wouldn't have seen half the sights we have and done half the things we've done. She's the epitome of adventure."

"I'll give you that," Maude laughed. "Speak of the devil, here she comes."

"Oh Opal, how was it?" Ruby asked.

"It was dazzling," Opal smiled. "I'm glad I made the trip up there. I can't explain it, but there's something special about this place."

"We're glad you enjoyed your time taking it all in," Ruby nodded. "Want a donut? There's one left with your name on it!"

"Don't mind if I do," Opal laughed. "Thank you."

"Alright, we better head back to the hotel if we're going to have time to dress and get refreshed before the show tonight," Ruby said.

"Let's change quickly and get this show on the road," Opal beamed. "I just know it's going to be an evening to remember!"

Chapter Twelve

"Where exactly is this place you're taking us to tonight?" Ruby asked Opal. She was rummaging through her suitcase for something suitable to wear.

"It's in the Village," Opal said, standing back to admire herself in the mirror. "This is going to knock them all dead." Opal, as usual, had gone all out for the occasion. She was wearing her best evening gown, bejeweled with sapphire rhinestones. She had an ivory feather boa draped across her shoulders. The outfit was topped off by her prized possession, a tiara that came out for all formal events.

"A tiara, really?" Maude asked. "You look like, well, I'm not even going to say her name."

Ruby looked quickly at Opal and winced.

"And it's in a village? Then why are we dressing up?" Maude asked. "A village doesn't sound all that classy."

Opal shook her head in disbelief. "Honestly, Maude. Sometimes I wonder how it is that all my fashion advice has never taken hold. We're dressing up because we're going to a show. All the stars will be there. Ricky said it's divine!"

"It's a pity he couldn't join us. I would have liked to have seen him," Ruby said. She held a blouse against her body and studied the look in the mirror. It didn't look right, so she threw it aside and grabbed another.

"I know. I was hoping to see him too, but his roommate got a deal on some last-minute tickets to Bermuda. Honestly, he works so hard, he really needed the time away," Opal said.

"What's he doing again?" Maude asked.

"He works with one of the costumers down in the theater district. He's working with all the really big names. I always said he'd go far. He has a flair for that kind of thing. That's probably why we got along so well, two likeminded people with an insatiable love of beauty," Opal twirled her feather boa around her neck. "This was one of the boas he gave me. He said Elizabeth Taylor wore it one time."

Maude cut a quick look at Ruby before finally settling on an outfit to wear for the evening.

Opal took one look at the clothes Maude was holding and snatched them away. "You can't be serious!

"Hey!" Maude yelled.

"Here, let me find you something," Opal went to her bag and began digging through outfits that would accentuate Maude's broader assets.

The taxi ride to the theatre was uneventful, which as Maude pointed out as they stood in line for the show, was an event in itself. Ricky had certainly recommended a popular spot. The line quickly began to wrap around the building.

"Glad we got here early," Maude said as she looked around at the crowd forming.

"It looks like it's moving quickly," Ruby supposed.

A few minutes later they were standing in front of the ticket booth.

"Hi, we'd like three tickets for tonight's show," Opal began.

The man in the booth didn't look up. "You want a table or want to sit at the bar?"

"Oh, we definitely want a table. The closer to the stage the better," Opal began. "My friend, Ricky McNeal, he really is a dream you know, he said this was the best show in town and that we simply couldn't miss it for the world. He wanted to join us but he's out of town at the moment, so it's just the three of us and the show of a lifetime."

The man looked up and studied her closely. He was wearing a suit of sorts, with blue slacks held up by a red belt and suspenders, a white shirt, and a vibrant canary yellow blazer. The ensemble was highlighted by a blue tie with tiny red hearts loosely tied around his neck. He lowered his glasses and studied Opal over the frames. "What's your name?"

"Opal Tyler," Opal smiled brightly.

"I wondered. Ricky mentioned that he had a darling friend that might stop by here sometime. Ooh, Destiny is going to love you!" he told her. He turned and snapped his fingers at someone standing in the shadows who instantly appeared beside him. "Take them to table number four. Tell Destiny they're friends of Ricky and they want a night to remember."

They were ushered to a table directly in front of the stage. Before they could take their seats, a tall woman swept past everyone else in the room to saddle right up to Opal.

"You must be the famous Opal that Ricky is always talking about," she wrapped her arms around Opal and gave her a giant hug. "You are every bit as fabulous as he always said." She let Opal go and waved her arm around the room. "I'm Destiny. If you need anything, anything at all, just let one of the staff know. Ricky's one of our favorites and he told us that his darling Opal deserves the absolute best!"

She was gone as quickly as she had arrived only to be replaced by their waiter.

"Good evening, ladies. I'm Stephen. I'll be your waiter tonight," he began. "What can I get you to drink?"

Maude ordered a soda while Ruby and Opal both ordered water.

"What kind of place is this?" Maude asked after their waiter had walked over to another table.

"Ricky said it's fabulous," Opal said, waving her hand to brush away Maude's concern.

"Is that Cher?" Ruby whispered to Opal.

Maude turned and looked. "Well, it was when she was with Sonny, but the current Cher is walking through the front door." Maude motioned to the door with her thumb.

Before they could contemplate the sudden appearance of multiple Chers, Destiny pulled up a chair and sat down next to Opal.

"So, I know you're Opal," she patted Opal's hand like they'd known each other for years. "Now let me see if I can guess the rest of this trio. You," she pointed at Ruby, "have an aura of class and sophistication. A real Southern gentlewoman. You must be Ruby."

Ruby smiled and patted her hair. "Yes. That's right."

Destiny gave a knowing smile. "Now you," she looked at Maude, "you look like a real spitfire who has never succumbed to the societal pressures of fashion and decorum. With that much gumption, you've got to be Maude."

Maude nodded, not completely sure she was receiving a compliment.

"It's so wonderful to finally meet you. Ricky is such a doll. He's told me all about you of course. He told me you were coming to the city while he was out of town and if you got the chance to stop by that I was to treat you like royalty. Spare no expense! You gals are in for a glorious night. We've got something special a little later on, as you can probably tell from all the girls walking around, but I won't say anything else right now. Don't want to spoil all the surprises," she winked at them. She was gone as quickly as she arrived.

The waiter brought the drinks and asked for their orders.

"I'd like the Caesar salad, please," Opal told him.

"I'll have the beef to start," Maude said. "Whatever kind of beef you have."

"Oh honey, we have the beef," he winked.

"Oh, that sounds good. I think I'll have that, too," Ruby said, handing the menu back to him. "And would you mind bringing me a soda or an iced tea as well? Whatever you have. I feel like splurging tonight."

Ruby turned to Opal who was admiring the stage. "Ricky did this. I can tell," Opal said.

Maude nudged the waiter before he could get away. "Can you refill my soda, but this time add a little Jack to it?" She asked.

He winked and was off to the kitchen.

"You have an excellent eye!" Destiny was back at Opal's side in time to hear the comment about Ricky. "Almost as soon as Ricky got into town, he was here revamping the set. He's a gem, that one."

"He certainly is. I just love him to death. He's definitely one of a kind," Opal agreed.

Destiny and Opal chatted about Ricky and all the changes he had suggested to the show. Opal told her about the sellout performances his shows always brought to the theater and how he could turn the mundane into the extraordinary. They both agreed that it would be amazing if he could get a show of his own, but he seemed happy working in an area that allowed him to have an influence over many shows at once.

The waiter returned with an appetizer and the drinks Maude and Ruby had ordered.

"Compliments of the house," he said as he put the steaming hot bowl in front of them. "It's our special bean dip. No one can resist it. It keeps everyone coming back for more." He quickly sat down a basket of chips.

"This looks delicious," Ruby said. She took one of the chips and scooped a liberal amount of dip.

"Sure does," Maude followed suit.

"Eat up, ladies," Destiny said. She helped herself to the chips and dip. "This stuff is my favorite!"

She and Opal continued discussing Ricky and his success in the Big Apple while Ruby and Maude ate the appetizer in front of them.

After she had eaten a few chips, Ruby turned and whispered to Maude, "This stuff is a little spicy, isn't it? Kinda sneaks up on you," Ruby said.

"You ain't kidding," Maude whispered back. She picked up her glass of soda and drank half of it in one gulp.

Ruby followed suit by drinking a large portion of her own drink. She looked at the glass suspiciously. "Does your drink taste funny?" she whispered to Maude.

Before Maude could answer, she continued. "Must be the way they make tea up here that adds a little flavor. Maybe the water or something," Ruby said. She smacked her lips trying to decide if she liked the flavor or not.

"That's my cue," Destiny sprang up from her seat as the band started to play. She looked quickly at the almost empty bowl of dip. "And I have Carlos bring out some more chips and dip. I'm so glad you liked it. And you need a refill on your drinks. Enjoy the show. See you gals afterwards. Tata!"

Ruby was finishing the last of her drink. She turned to Opal, "That's so nice of her to give us this. It really is delicious, but be careful, Opal. It can sneak up on you."

"She's great," Opal said, helping herself to the last of the appetizer. "It's nice to have another professional to talk to."

A few minutes later, Carlos sat a fresh basket of chips and a new bowl of dip in front of the Stone Sisters. The drinks were replenished as well. Ruby, whose tongue was still on fire from the first round of dip, wasted no time in finishing her drink.

"You know," Ruby smacked her lips and turned to Maude, "I'm starting to get used to this strange taste up here. It's not that bad."

"Good evening, all you fabulous people out there!" Destiny's voice boomed from the stage. "We have a marvelous show for you tonight, because as you know, we are all good times and love for our fellow man," she gave the audience a sideways glance and wink. "Or woman."

The audience roared with applause.

"This is exciting," Ruby giggled.

"None of you fool me. I know what kind of crowd we have here tonight." Destiny pointed to the tables on the left. "We have many types of saints and sinners!" She swept her arm dramatically across the room to include everyone present.

The noise of the crowd was deafening. Ruby, Maude, and Opal could hardly believe the excitement in the room. Destiny gave Opal a little wink as if to say this was only the beginning.

"Who's ready to spend an evening with the greatest divas of all time?" Destiny practically had to yell into the microphone to be heard over the audience.

"This place is about to go nuts!" Maude yelled to Ruby and Opal.

"Then let's have a big round of applause for the Divine Miss M, herself, Bette Midler!" Destiny said.

"Oh my goodness, I love her!" Ruby exclaimed.

"I didn't know she was that tall," Maude said.

"It's the heels," Opal assured her.

"I don't know," Maude stared up at the stage. "From here she looks to be about six foot five."

"Maude, you really don't know anything about show business. The right heels and lighting angles can make all the difference," Opal explained knowingly.

Ruby wasn't listening. She was too busy singing along to The Rose. "I always loved this song," she hummed.

"What in the world has gotten into you, Ruby?" Maude asked as the tall diva left the stage.

"My lovelies, boy do we have a special treat this evening! Welcome back, Ms. Dolly!" Destiny cheered from the stage.

"Dolly! Y'all know I love me some Dolly!" Ruby cheered.

"She's enjoying herself, Maude. That's what happens when people truly immerse themselves in live theater. I've been trying to tell you that for years," Opal leaned over and said.

"Well, I'm about to immerse myself in this food," Maude replied as Carlos brought out the main entrees.

He cleared the empty glasses and appetizer before he replaced each lady's drink. "Enjoy ladies," he said.

"This looks yummy," Ruby said with a grin.

Maude watched Ruby more closely. She certainly was acting odd.

"Isn't she marvelous, folks!" Destiny was back on stage to introduce Barbra Streisand who brought the house down when she sang You Don't Bring Me Flowers Anymore.

"Now," Destiny was back on stage. She was quieting the audience down with a wave of her hands. "I have it on great authority that we have a birthday boy here tonight," she said. A spotlight shown on a man three tables away. "We can't let the night go by without wishing you a very special birthday!"

Marilyn Monroe walked out onto the stage and performed a very sultry rendition of the happy birthday song. Before she was finished, she sauntered down to his table and planted a kiss on top of his forehead. Candy apple red lipstick glistened off his bald head.

"Isn't this fun! They brought out a Marilyn impersonator to sing happy birthday to him," Ruby giggled.

Ruby was halfway finished with her third drink of the night. She was swaying happily along with the melody. Maude watched her even more closely. While Ruby was watching Marilyn singing the final bars of her song, Maude picked up Ruby's glass and smelled it. Her eyes almost crossed. She poured the rest of Ruby's drink into her own glass and frowned.

"Oh my," Ruby said, looking down at her glass. "My drink is empty again."

"You sure have been thirsty," Maude said quickly.

"The stuff up here sure is funny. It makes you all light headed and everything," Ruby said.

"It can," Maude agreed. "I'll get you another drink," Maude assured Ruby.

"Good because I'm really thirsty," Ruby told her.

Maude waved to Carlos. "I'm not sure what you gave her, but it's full of alcohol! I can smell it from here!" Maude whispered furiously.

"She asked for a soda or an iced tea," he squeaked. "She said she wanted to splurge!"

"Exactly!" Maude snapped. "What did you bring her?"

"A vodka soda and then two Long Island Iced Teas," he whimpered.

"Oh dear God!" Maude grimaced. "You got the deacon's wife drunk! Do not bring back any alcohol to this table. Plain water or plain soda only this time," she said sternly and handed him their glasses.

He scurried away without a word.

∽ Chapter Thirteen ∽

After a brief intermission, a new duo took the stage, to the thrill of the crowd. Opal stood up and clapped loudly while Ruby nearly passed out from excitement.

"Oh my heavens, look who it is! And she's wearing the ruby slippers!" Ruby screamed gleefully.

"I could've sworn she died twenty or some odd years ago," Maude said.

"Shh, you're killing my vibe," Opal whispered. "And Ruby's too."

"I don't think anyone can get close to Ruby's vibe right now," Maude said under her breath as the lyrics to Cabaret were sung by an off-key Liza Minelli and Judy Garland.

"Judy is about sixty pounds heavier and when did Liza become black?" Maude asked.

"Gotta be the lighting," Ruby said in a haze. "Mother and daughter reunited. What a sweet time it is to be alive."

"I don't reckon Judy is," Maude started to say, but Ruby shushed her.

After Liza and Judy cleared the stage, the entire area was suddenly filled with darkness. From the back, several people began to cheer, but nothing seemed to be happening. Maude could faintly make out the silhouettes of people moving in front of her, but she couldn't tell what exactly was happening. The crowd was growing more restless by the second. They began clapping in unison, slowly at first and then faster as the level of anticipation rose to a new height.

Then they heard music from offstage. The applause grew more feverish.

"If I could turn back time!" a voice blared through the room.

The crowd was uncontrollable as Cher stepped through the center curtain in a fishnet outfit that would have been illegal in Rhinestone. She donned a sailor's cap atop her jet-black hair. She strutted across the stage making sure each section got a moment of her attention. The audience ate it up. Before she started the last chorus, she tossed the hat into the crowd. Several tables scuffled to grab it in midair.

"Welcome!" Cher said when the music had ended and the applause died down. "To the Cher-est show on earth!"

Ruby stood up and cheered. "Woohoo!" She twirled her napkin over her head and beamed.

Maude stood up and gently pushed her back down into her seat.

"Wow, Ruby. I never knew you liked Cher so much," Opal said watching her.

"I can turn back time," Ruby sang happily. "Oops, I think I messed up," she giggled.

"She certainly seems to be in the spirit of things," Maude said behind her napkin to Opal.

Ruby knew a surprising number of recent Cher hits. She sang along and even added a few dance moves of her own. Two guys sitting at the table beside them jumped up and took turns dancing with her to the delight of all those around them.

"Care to join us?" Opal jumped up and looked at Maude who shook her head.

"I think I'll stay right here," she said.

The tempo changed to some of Cher's earlier hits. She waved to the audience and exited on the left side of the stage. The curtain was still waving when Cher re-entered the stage on the right, this time wearing an outfit straight out of the 1960s. She was wearing hip hugger red, blue, and yellow stripes. Her shirt was blindingly bright yellow topped with a faux fur fringe vest. Around her head, she wore a string of beads that tied at the back and hung loosely down the side of her head.

"That was fast!" Ruby said with a slight slur.

"Sure was," Maude agreed.

"You have to be quick in theater," Opal said knowingly. She had taken the opportunity to sit down and have a drink of water during the costume change.

"Quick is one thing, but why is she shorter?" Maude asked.

"And her nose is different," Ruby added. "Probably the lighting again."

"I'm sure it's the lighting," Opal winked.

"And now, I need some help with a little duet I started out with," Cher announced as soon as she'd finished her Dark Lady number. "Who wants to be my Sonny tonight?"

The audience erupted. Opal stood up to march onstage, but Ruby, swept up in the excitement of the moment, pushed her back down and began jumping up and down.

"Me! Me!" Ruby yelled. "Pick me! Pick me!"

"Oh yes! The cute little darling in the front row. Come on up here, gorgeous," Cher said.

"Oh dear God," Maude gasped.

"Ruby's days of playing backup dancer are over," giggled Opal.

"Where're ya from, darling?" Cher asked.

"Rhinestone," Ruby answered in a distinctive Southern drawl.

"Oh my goodness, will you listen to that accent!" Cher said. The crowd cheered with more than a few cat whistles.

"You ready to do this thing?" Cher asked.

Ruby nodded seriously.

Cher hugged her around the shoulders. "Don't be nervous, sugar."

"I'm not nervous at all," Ruby hiccupped.

The music started and Cher sang the first few lines. When Sonny's part started, she thrust the microphone in front of Ruby.

"Babe," Ruby said.

Cher looked a little confused, but shook it off quickly. She sang Sonny's part, and then her own before putting the microphone back in front of Ruby for Sonny's next few lines.

"Babe," Ruby said again, in a low voice.

The crowd cheered.

Cher smiled. She sang a few lines, then once again, the microphone was back in front of Ruby.

"Babe," Ruby said for the third time, but this time her voice was a bit higher.

"Is that the only word you know?" Cher asked.

"Maybe," Ruby smiled.

The crowd roared with laughter. Cher was almost doubled over laughing at her singing partner. She stood up quickly. "Okay, here we go, let's do this thing," Cher said.

Cher sang a few words before letting Ruby add the one word she knew. It didn't even matter where Ruby's part came in. The crowd was so loud that most people couldn't hear the music anywhere.

"Ruby's changed. What on earth has gotten into her tonight?" Opal asked, completely stunned by her friend's eccentric behavior.

"Vodka and gin," Maude mumbled.

Opal stared at her in disbelief as Maude explained what had happened.

"Oh my stars," Opal whispered. "You got Ruby drunk!"

"I didn't get her drunk. The waiter did. He's the one who gave her those," Maude explained.

"You know Ruby doesn't drink!" Opal said.

"I know," Maude began to explain, but Opal cut her off.

"And you got her drunk!" Opal continued.

"I didn't get her drunk," Maude stammered.

"Oh Maude, this is too much," Opal shook her head. "How could you do that to sweet little innocent Ruby?"

"I didn't have anything to do with it! I didn't get her drunk," Maude said. "I didn't even realize it at first."

"How could you do that to Ruby?" Opal continued, shaking her head in disbelief.

"I didn't do anything," Maude stammered again, although she was starting to feel much guiltier than she had before.

"Exactly," Opal said as though the matter was settled. "You should have done something."

"I did as soon as I realized what was going on. I told him to stop giving her alcohol, but it was too late," Maude said.

"Well, I hope you're proud of yourself," Opal crossed her arms. "She's on a whole other planet right about now."

"It was only a few glasses," Maude whispered.

"A few glasses for a teetotaler is like a whole barrel." Opal hissed.

"I know," Maude wailed. She looked over at Ruby who was wide-eyed and grinning unlike ever before.

"Let's have a huge round of applause for tonight's Sonny!" Cher yelled.

Ruby gave a long, low bow before returning to the table with Opal and Maude.

"What a night," she breathed and drained Opal's water glass. "I feel amazing."

"Oh, um, sure Ruby, you can have it. Water's probably what you need actually," Opal said.

Before Maude or Opal could explain to Ruby what had happened, the unmistakable rhythms of disco filled the air. Multicolored lights swirled throughout the audience and stage. Cher danced to the music for a few beats and then exited to the left of the stage. No sooner had the last beads on her head passed the curtain did she reappear on the right, this time wearing a foxy full length gold bodysuit.

"Take me home," Cher belted out.

"Woo!" Ruby yelled. She stood up and danced with the guys at the table beside them.

"I didn't know she knew how to disco," Opal said.

"She doesn't," Maude said.

Ruby was now bumping hips with a man on either side of her. The man on her right took her hand and twirled her around. When she had stopped spinning, the gentleman on her left began to lead her around in a modified version of the hustle. Ruby was having the time of her life and he seemed to be too intoxicated to realize she'd stepped on his foot four different times.

She continued dancing with both of them while Cher sang through a montage of several more of her biggest hits.

There was a change in tempo. A keyboard solo played offstage. Cher stood behind the microphone, "Don't you know," she began to sing.

Ruby said goodbye to her new friends and stumbled back over to Maude and Ruby.

"What a time it is to be alive!" Ruby cheered.

"You looked like you were having a great time," Opal said.

"I am," Ruby said. "Is it hot in here? Who cares!"

Just then Cher broke into the chorus of I Found Someone. The crowd roared as the two previous Chers came from either side of the stage to join her at the microphone. They continued singing as Dolly, Bette, and Barbra walked out on stage to thundering applause. Liza and Judy were the last to join the ensemble. Maude, Opal, and Ruby could hardly hear the music for the roar of the crowd even though they were only feet from the stage. When the music ended, the performers held hands and took a long bow to the audience. The applause lasted more than a minute.

"Maybe I'm drunk too, because I'm seeing three of them," Maude rubbed her eyes and stared again into the bright lights.

"What a night," Ruby repeated over and over again. By this time, she had sunk back into her chair and began fanning herself with a folded museum program she had fished out of her purse.

The three Chers disappeared, along with Judy, Liza, Dolly, Barbra, and Bette. Destiny returned to the stage again and asked for another round of applause for all of the amazing performers. "Don't forget next Friday is our anniversary show! Tina Turner will be making a surprise appearance! All these divas for the price of one. Reminds me of my youth!"

The crowd cheered and the main lights overhead turned on. People began clearing out from the tables, leaving stacks of money behind.

"Oooh, darlings, how was everything? And what a set of pipes on you, Ruby!" Destiny gushed. She sank down in the empty chair next to Ruby and grinned. Ruby blushed and drank some more water.

"I'm so tired, but I don't think I'll ever be able to sleep. This was amazing! Dolly and Barbra and even Judy! I can't even believe it!" Ruby exclaimed.

"Well, believe it sister!" Destiny howled. "I need to go check on things backstage and then skedaddle on out of this here dress, but yall take your time and it was so good to meet you. Y'all come back now ya here!"

Maude, Ruby, and Opal all left a generous tip on the table and gathered up their things.

"No one is going to believe what a night we've had," Ruby whooped.

"They will when they see all of the pictures I took," Opal smiled.

"I wouldn't be showing all of these pictures," Maude cautioned.

"Let's get you back to the hotel, Ruby," Opal smiled. "You've had quite the night."

"I'll never forget it," Ruby said dreamily.

"I'm not so sure about that," Maude mumbled.

The taxi driver got an earful on the drive back to the Plaza. By the end of the ride, he had learned all about Ruby's time on stage and the songs they had all sung.

"Oh, I've been there. Liz Taylor is there on Thursdays. You should hit the club up then!" he said.

"We love her," Ruby replied.

"There's a Madonna one too some nights," he added. "You should see the cones on that one."

"Well, that is inappropriate!" Ruby snapped and pulled her shawl tighter around her neck.

"What?" the driver asked. "I'm just saying. He paid good money for those, ya know. You can get 'em at any gag shop around here. His name's Roger and he works over on Broadway as a swing."

"As a what?" Maude asked.

"A swing over on Broadway," the driver said. "You know, an offstage performer who only goes on if someone in the ensemble is unable to do so."

"They are so uncultured," Opal sighed. "Anyway, this is us. Thanks for the lift! Alright, easy Ruby, I'll get your purse." She gave Maude a sharp look and shook her head.

Maude paid the driver and followed behind Opal who was supporting Ruby up the steps. Opal turned to look at Maude and whispered sharply, "This was you just the other night, and now you've brought Ruby down with you. I swear, I cannot take y'all anywhere."

Once they got to their room, Opal ran Ruby a shower and helped her out of her jewelry. "God, I hope she doesn't drown in there," Opal sighed. "She's going to kill you tomorrow."

"Maybe she won't remember," Maude offered fretfully.

"When she wakes up feeling like she was hit by the subway train, you get to tell her what happened," Opal said ruefully. "I'm not about to get on the bad side of Ruby Montgomery. No ma'am, no thank you."

"Why's it always gotta be me?" Maude huffed.

"You just attract trouble," Opal laughed. She pressed her ear against the bathroom door and heard Ruby singing a very off-key version of Somewhere Over the Rainbow.

"Is she ok?" Maude asked.

"She's still kickin'," Opal said. "She's going to be feeling somewhat under the rainbow tomorrow."

Maude grimaced and bit her bottom lip. "Maybe it won't be that bad. She's had a glass of wine before. A few times actually."

Opal laughed out loud and shook her head. "Those glasses of wine are more like grape juice compared to those heavy-handed bartenders tonight. She'll get over it, though she might not feel like going to the amusement park tomorrow. Oh Lordy, here she comes."

Ruby emerged from the bathroom in her silk pajamas with her hair wrapped up in a towel. Opal reminded her where her toothbrush was and gave her some medicine for her headache that was sure to come in the morning. After Ruby was ready for bed, Maude quickly ducked into the bathroom and shut the door behind her.

"Opal, I'm suddenly exhausted. I think I need to go to sleep," Ruby yawned. Before Opal could reply, Ruby was sound asleep across the first bed snoring.

~Chapter Fourteen~

The next morning, Ruby moaned and groaned from under the pile of pillows. "I have the worst headache," Ruby grimaced as she rubbed her head. "I feel like my whole body is going to explode."

"I'm not surprised," Opal said. She was halfway through her morning stretches when Ruby mumbled from underneath the covers of her bed.

"What's that supposed to mean?" Ruby mumbled. "I feel like I've been hit by a train."

"Why don't you ask Maude," Opal said innocently. She stretched her arms high over her head and then pulled her body into an obscure yoga pose.

Maude glared at her and shook her head slightly.

"What's Opal talking about, Maude?" Ruby asked, barely lifting her head off the pillow.

Maude took a deep breath before turning her attention to Ruby. "There seems to have been a mix-up last night with our drinks."

"What?" Ruby asked.

"Maude got you drunk," Opal said standing up from her final stretch of the morning. "Now I feel so much better after all that stretching. You two should join me tomorrow morning. Yoga really opens up the body and soul."

"Wait a minute. You what?" Ruby looked up at Maude before quickly laying her head back on the pillow.

"I did not get her drunk," Maude said to Opal. She turned to Ruby to explain, "I did not get you drunk. I ordered Jack and Coke and the waiter misunderstood and thought you also wanted alcohol, so you got a few vodka sodas and some Long Islands."

"Is that why it tasted funny?" Ruby asked.

"Yep, that's the reason," Maude said.

"But," Ruby started again.

"I still don't know why in the world you let her drink it," Opal said. "You know Ruby doesn't drink."

"I know she doesn't drink," Maude said emphatically. "I didn't know she an actual drink until it was too late."

"Likely story," Opal huffed. "You're just lucky Ruby survived the night. Anything could have happened to her. She could have been abducted."

"Abducted?" Ruby squealed.

"Abducted?" Maude said, a little more loudly than she meant to. "How could she have been abducted? We were together at a show. It's not like she was in a coma in a dark alleyway somewhere."

"Oh, my head," Ruby mumbled. "Will someone please explain to me what's going on!"

"What about those two men she was dancing with? They looked very suspicious to me," Opal said with a nod of her head as though her argument was ironclad.

"The ones doing the Hustle?" Maude asked in disbelief.

"What a minute," Ruby raised her head again. "I danced with some men?"

"Yeah, you did the Hustle, but not very well. We really need to work on your moves before we come back up here," Opal said, turning her attention to Ruby.

"Oh my goodness. What is Jameson going to think?" Ruby laid back down. Her hand was still massaging her temple.

"That Maude was trying to kill you!" Opal said.

"I wasn't trying to kill anybody!" Maude replied.

Ruby groaned from the bed again and buried her face in her pillow. "I'm never leaving the house again."

"You see what you've done to Ruby," Opal continued. "First you get her drunk, then you let her do awful dance moves with strangers, and you potentially got her abducted. I just can't with this recklessness anymore."

Maude turned to pick up her clothes. "I'm getting a shower. You are way too dramatic about all this."

"But I have more questions!" Ruby wailed.

"Ask Opal," Maude snapped, before disappearing into the bathroom.

"I can't believe it," Ruby whimpered. She pulled the pillow over her face and sighed.

"Well, believe it," Opal laughed. "Oh, come on, Ruby. It wasn't that bad. I just like yanking Maude's chain. You had a great time and you'll never see any of those people again anyway."

"I really danced with strangers?" Ruby asked.

"I wouldn't exactly call it dancing, but for all intents and purposes, yes," Opal laughed.

"Oh no," Ruby whispered.

"And before you go fretting about that, it wasn't that big of a deal. You did some outdated disco moves with some new friends. You didn't cross any lines and you had a great time. I've got some stuff in my bag that will take that headache away in a jiffy," Opal explained. She rummaged through her bag underneath the table in the corner and found the two bottles she was looking for. "Here you go. Take a good swig of this one," she said, and handed her the small purple bottle.

"Are you sure?" Ruby asked.

"Absolutely," Opal assured her. Ruby took a swig from the bottle while Opal opened the larger pink bottle and dumped some of the mint green cream into her palms and began to rub the potion on the back of Ruby's neck. "That should do it. You'll be fine as wine in no time."

After a few minutes, Ruby had to admit that she did in fact feel much better. She was able to get out of bed and brush her damp hair before getting dressed for the day.

When Maude got out of the shower, she was surprised to see Ruby drinking a cup of coffee from the downstairs lobby.

"As soon as you're ready, Maude, we can head out," Opal said. "As usual, we're waiting on you."

"What? How in the world? Ruby, you were just practically bedridden twenty minutes ago," Maude stuttered.

"Ruby has an iron stomach. I guess some people can hold their liquor better than others," Opal winked. "Now hurry on up."

Maude threw on some clothes and ran a brush through her short hair. She settled for a ball cap that had been crumpled at the bottom of her suitcase. She sprayed on some perfume and followed Ruby and Opal out to the elevator.

"So, what's first on the agenda?" Maude asked.

"I figure we can eat on the boardwalk, do some people watching, sunbathe after we play in the waves, and then ride some rides," Opal suggested.

"Play in the waves? Sunbathe?" Maude gasped.

"Opal, it's too cold for that," Ruby agreed.

Opal merely shrugged and waved them off. "Well, if you two are too afraid of a little chill in the air."

"And what kind of rides?" Maude asked as the elevator spit them out in the lobby. "I haven't been on a rollercoaster in over a decade."

"Everybody rides the Cyclone when they come to Coney Island," Opal began. "It's tradition."

"I don't know about tradition," Maude said. She climbed into the taxi cab that Opal had expertly hailed and watched the buildings fly by through the window.

When they arrived near the infamous boardwalk, Ruby, Maude, and Opal tumbled out of the cab and took in the view. They breathed in the chilly salty air and marveled at the crowds of people going in all directions.

"This reminds me of the county fair over in Junction," Maude said. "They've got that big wheel and everything."

"I don't think the fair has a roller coaster like that," Ruby said with wide eyes.

"That thing doesn't look too safe," Maude stared up at the wooden roller coaster a little closer.

"It's perfectly fine, Maude," Opal said. "It wouldn't have lasted so long if it wasn't safe."

Maude looked over at her. "Just how old is this thing?"

"The sign at the entrance said it was built in 1927," Ruby mentioned.

Maude continued to look between her two friends and the giant structure. "I don't think I want to ride that."

"We're all going to ride it together," Opal said emphatically. "And then I'll get you some of their famous taffy for being a big girl."

Maude groaned audibly and rolled her eyes. "Well, y'all are not going to kill me on an empty stomach. Let's find somewhere to eat."

"You're not going to eat a bunch and then throw it up on the ride," Opal said.

"But I'm hungry. I haven't eaten anything since last night," Maude grumbled.

"I don't think it's a good idea to eat a big lunch, but I am a little hungry, too," Ruby offered. "Maybe we could grab a bite to eat and then ride something a little milder before we ride the roller coaster."

Opal shrugged. "Okay, but don't wait too long or the lines will wrap all the way to New Jersey."

Maude wasn't listening. She had already spotted Nathan's Famous and was heading in that direction.

The smells of the iconic hotdog acted like a siren's song to her hungry belly.

"Hotdogs?" Opal asked. "That's not going to be pretty in a little while."

Ruby and Opal caught up with Maude a moment later. It was already crowded.

"We'll be lucky to find a spot to sit down," Maude mentioned.

"We can always take them to the beach," Opal offered.

"I ain't going to a frozen beach and riding a rollercoaster all in one afternoon," Maude huffed.

"Why don't you go find a table while Opal and I order?" Ruby suggested.

Maude looked at Opal carefully. "I don't trust her with my food."

"Nonsense, Maude. I'll do the ordering," Ruby assured her. "What do you want?"

"A hotdog is a hotdog. Just get me one of their famous footlong ones," Maude said. "Well, I am pretty hungry. Better make it two."

"Are you sure?" Ruby asked. "That's two feet."

"Yep," Maude said as she walked away to find a table. "And don't you try anything funny, Opal," she yelled over her shoulder.

It was several more minutes before Ruby and Opal made it to the counter.

"What can I get ya?" the gruff looking man asked Ruby.

"I think I'll just have a chili dog and some cheese fries," Ruby said. "And Maude said she wants two of your famous hotdogs."

"Everything on 'em," the man grunted.

Ruby turned to Opal. "Do you think Maude wants fries?"

"Of course, she does," Opal replied.

The man nodded, hearing Opal's response.

"And she wants some cheese fries as well," Ruby said.

He nodded again and looked at Opal. "And for you?"

"I'll take some of your fried vegetables. I don't eat meat," Opal smiled.

"Alright," he nodded. "Three drinks?"

Opal nodded and turned to Ruby and smiled sweetly. "I think that'll cover it."

They found Maude at a table not far from the entrance.

Maude looked at the tray before her. "What is this?"

"It's the hotdogs you ordered," Ruby said pleasantly.

"What's all that stuff on it?" Maude asked.

"Looks like it's got some grilled onions and green peppers," Ruby said helpfully.

"And there's a pickle on top of the chili," Opal said, examining Maude's lunch. "Oh, and it looks like you've got some sauerkraut and mustard on there. That looks like the good kind of mustard, too. It's nice and tangy."

"I told you not to let Opal order for me," Maude grumbled.

"I didn't," Opal said sweetly.

"I ordered for you," Ruby grimaced.

"You ordered this, Ruby?" Maude said in disbelief.

"I told him to give me two of the famous ones," Ruby explained.

"That is what you said, Maude," Opal added.

"I didn't know what it came with," Ruby squeaked.

"But Opal, you know I don't eat this stuff. I just wanted two regular old hotdogs," Maude protested.

"You said I couldn't order for you, so I didn't want to go against your orders," Opal smiled.

"Somehow I think this is revenge for last night," Maude grumbled.

"It's no such thing," Ruby huffed. "I ordered the famous ones that you said. You got exactly what you asked for. Now, stop with all this mess and eat them," Ruby said with more gusto than she normally used.

"Oh alright. Fine," Maude said, without looking up at either of them.

They all fell into silence as they began to eat their lunch.

"You know," Maude said, when she had finished the first one. "This thing ain't half bad."

"So I see," Ruby laughed.

"What?" Maude asked.

"You inhaled the first one," Opal said.

"It was good," Maude said. She licked some of the chili off her fingers.

"Maude!" Ruby was aghast. "Don't do that."

"What?" Maude asked again. A dollop of chili dribbled down chin which she wiped off with the back of her hand.

"Don't lick your fingers," Ruby looked mortified. "That is so rude, and not to mention unladylike. Have some couth."

"Don't want to waste any," Maude said.

"She never was mistaken for a lady," Opal said under her breath.

Maude glared at her and began to eat her fries.

"Here's another napkin. You have food all down your shirt," Ruby sighed. "I swear, it's like eating with Mavis sometimes."

"Those fried vegetables weren't bad," Opal said. "Of course they weren't as good as what you make Ruby, but they weren't half bad."

"Now about that taffy," Maude interjected.

"On second thought, I don't think taffy will be good for your teeth," Opal countered.

"But you said earlier!" Maude began.

"I think Opal is right on this one," Ruby nodded. "That taffy will stick to our teeth and it's liable to pull them out."

"No one of us have dentures," Maude grumbled, but she knew it was a losing battle. "I'll get some on the way out if I want to," she said to herself.

They threw away their trash and gathered up their purses. "Now about that coaster," Opal said gleefully.

"Let's do something a little tamer before we think about tackling that one," Ruby suggested. "My stomach is still settling and I don't want my headache to come back either."

"Do you need another dose?" Opal asked. "I brought my bottles with me just in case."

"I think I'm ok for now," Ruby smiled.

"That Ferris wheel looking thing looks safe," Maude pointed out. "I bet the views are amazing. Come on!"

"But Ruby doesn't like heights," Opal reminded her.

"It's ok," Ruby said stoically. "This is a once in a lifetime experience. I'll do it."

"Atta girl," Maude beamed. She slapped Ruby on the back. "Deno's Wonder Wheel? Deno, hmm. I wonder if he's related to Eileen from the Auxiliary. She had an ex-husband named Deno, remember?"

"Yes, Maude, everyone with the same first name is related," Opal said sarcastically. "Do you ever do any research about places you visit? This is one of the oldest rides at the park. It was bought by a man named Deno a few years ago, so he renamed it. It's still the same iconic wheel though from the beginning."

"Not everyone is a walking encyclopedia," Maude huffed.

"It stands one hundred and fifty feet tall," Opal continued.

"That's fifteen stories!" Ruby gasped.

"Exactly," Opal nodded. "Look at that cart right there," she pointed. "Some of them swing kinda, and some of them don't. Come on, we can all ride in one car together."

"On second thought," Ruby stuttered, but Opal and Maude ahead already whisked her towards the giant wheel.

Unfortunately for Ruby, they were placed in one of the carts that moved. The swinging cart slid on a serpentine track towards the center of the wheel, and as the wheel rotated, the cart slid back towards the outer rim of the ride. Ruby closed her eyes the entire time in white knuckled her purse from inside the moving cart.

"Just breathe, Ruby. And when you're ready, take a look at this amazing view," Opal said patiently.

Ruby shook her head and held her breath for as long as she could. When the ride finally stopped to let them off, she flew out of the cart leaving Maude and Opal in her wake.

"I don't reckon she liked that one," Maude said.

"Well, it was her idea. She wanted something mild," Opal shrugged.

~Chapter Fifteen~

Once Ruby had calmed down, they decided to walk along the boardwalk for a bit. Maude bought them each a bag of salt water taffy from a vendor and kept all of her teeth in the process.

After once again talking Opal out of playing in the waves, Ruby decided that it was time to brave the infamous wooden roller coaster. The closer they got to the coaster, the more Maude became robotic. The line wasn't as long as they thought it would be, which made Maude even more nervous.

"It's going to be ok," Opal patted her shoulder. "No one has ever died on this ride. So, the odds are certainly in your favor. At least, I think that's right."

"That's not helping," Maude sighed.

"If something did happen, just imagine the headlines! I bet we'd make the Rhinestone Register and everything," Opal surmised.

"Just eat more of your taffy," Ruby encouraged Maude. She was looking a little green herself, but she soldiered on.

"You have got to be kidding me," a voice behind them suddenly cackled.

Maude gasped and clinched Ruby's hand. "This is it, I am in hell."

Opal turned on her heels and grinned wickedly. Nadine Waters was standing five people being them. "Well hello Nadine. Fancy seeing you here today."

"I was going to say the same thing about you all. It seems that we keep bumping into each other," Nadine agreed.

"It must be my magnetic personality," Opal shrugged. "Are you going to ride the Cyclone?"

"I wouldn't miss the opportunity! I love a good thrill!" Nadine smiled. "Though I am a bit surprised to see Maude in line for it."

"If I don't turn around, it'll be like she's not even there," Maude whispered to Ruby.

Nadine excused herself and moved closer towards Opal, Ruby, and Maude. "That's better. Felt like I was shouting," she smiled.

"Are you going to ride by yourself, Nadine?" Opal asked. "Maude and Ruby can ride together, and since we are both single riders, we could go together if you like?"

"I would love that!" Nadine answered. "It's always nice to experience things with people who can appreciate them."

Maude turned around and cut her eyes at her quickly. "Oh Maude, here's one of those wet wipes for you. You have something all over your shirt, and I'll be danged if it isn't on your chin as well. Let me help you." She scrubbed the front of Maude's shirt until she was satisfied with the process. In place of the stain was now a soaking wet circle in the center of her chest.

"Here's another wet wipe. Scrub that spot on your face," Nadine instructed.

"I did tell you," Ruby whispered to Maude who was silently seething.

As the line moved closer to the boarding platform, Maude began to sweat. But when they were the next group to board, Ruby was the one who suddenly jumped out of line.

Maude, Opal, and Nadine looked at each other and quickly followed her to the side away from the line.

"What is going on, Ruby?" Maude croaked.

Ruby fanned herself with some napkins that Opal found in her purse. "I think I need to keep my feet on the ground for a while," she whispered.

"The gentleman said he would hold our place in line for as long as you need. When you're ready, we can be the next group boarded," Nadine explained.

"I'm sorry, I don't think I can do this one," Ruby said.

"That's ok, Ruby," Opal said. "We'll meet you at the exit. Are you sure you're ok?"

The color had returned to her cheeks and she nodded. "I'm fine. I promise. Y'all have a great time. I'll try to snap your pictures on the way down!"

"If you two want to ride together, I'll ride alone," Opal offered.

Maude and Nadine both glared at her. "Never mind," Opal said sweetly. "Are you ok riding alone, Maude?"

"I think I'll go check on Ruby," Maude said.

"Not a chance, Maude," Nadine interrupted. She turned to a group of women and smiled. "Would one of you mind riding with our dear friend here? She is a little terrified and you look like you'd be the perfect partner for her."

"Of course!" the young woman agreed. She beamed at Maude and patted her on the back. "Oh my, I remember you! The Holy Father has blessed us on meeting again." She turned around to the group she had been standing with and clapped. "This is the lady Father Henry and I were telling you about from the plane!"

Maude suddenly recognized her as the young nun on the plane who had sung to her the entire flight from Atlanta to Washington DC. "Didn't you say you were singing at something or another in DC?"

"Oh, yes!" she squealed. "We sang at the National Cathedral and tomorrow we are singing at Saint Patrick's. It is a joyous honor."

"And riding a death trap is another joyous honor on your list?" Maude scoffed.

"There are people to witness to everywhere," she smiled back.

"I don't know how in the world I got talked into this mess," Maude mumbled as they waited for the next car to inch closer.

"Oh I just love the thrill of these things, don't you, Ms. Maude?" she asked.

Maude ignored her, but that didn't seem to deter the young nun's joyful spirit. She turned and began chatting with Opal and Nadine.

When the car stopped, they were ushered aboard by a young attendant. "Lower the bar securely over your lap," he ordered.

"This is going to be great!" Nadine cheered. She high-fived Opal and looked at Maude in front of her.

Maude reached up for the bar which seemed to only close halfway down. She glanced behind her at Opal whose safety bar was firmly in her lap.

"Wait a minute! This thing ain't closing all the way!" Maude yelled back for the attendant.

"It seems to be locked in place. It's not going anywhere," the nun reassured her. She ceased herself and whispered a quick prayer just to be sure.

"It ain't as far down as theirs. It ain't locked," Maude began to panic.

The attendant heard Maude's cries and came back to her car. He yanked the car up and down a couple of times to check it. "Looks fine," he yelled to someone down the line. Then he saw Maude's face. "But you don't. You gonna be okay?" he asked her.

Maude nodded more out of reflex than actual acknowledgement of the question.

"You good?" he asked her again.

Maude looked up at him with an ashen expression.

"Always put your faith in the Holy Father. He won't let anything happen to you," the nun patted Maude's hand which hadn't loosened the death grip on the safety bar.

"Give me a thumbs up if you're gonna make it," he told her.

With extreme effort, Maude allowed her thumb to straighten slightly. He took this as the go-ahead sign.

"We have a green one here. She's not gonna make it," he said as he walked away from Maude's car. "It's gonna get messy." He waved to his coworker down the line who must have started the car moving.

"Oh dear God!" Maude yelled as the car jerked forward and began the climb up the wooden structure.

"Yes, he will always ease our fears!" the nun yelled to her. She clearly didn't understand the level of Maude's discomfort.

Although Maude attended Beaver Crossing Holy Church for the Faithful most every Sunday, she was fairly certain that unless God himself was going to swoop down out of heaven and drop her safely on the ground in the next few minutes, they might be meeting much sooner than she wanted. "We're gonna die!" she screamed.

"Isn't this fun!" Nadine yelled behind Maude.

"Son of a!" Maude screamed as they crested the first peak of the ride.

"Wheeeeee!" Opal said. "This is amazing!"

Maude wasn't exactly sure which words she used or in what particular order she used them, but by the time their car pulled back into the exit, she was fairly certain that she had used all the adult words in her vocabulary multiple times. Her hair was disheveled and she looked like she had witnessed the rapture.

"That was a most unusual, ahem, prayer you recited," the nun said as they waited for their turn to exit. "I can honestly say I've never heard one quite so impassioned like that."

Maude was now trying to pry the bar open. "I can't get out! I can't get out!" she yelled. "This is a death trap!"

"Maude, you can't get out of the car until we get to the platform!" Opal said. "Act right!"

"I gotta get out of this thing!" Maude continued. "Lord, get me out of here!"

"It's going to be okay," the nun began to pat her arm again.

Maude turned to her. She looked like a deranged animal. "You don't know!"

"Maude, quit it!" Opal yelled from behind her. "You're embarrassing me."

"Opal's right. You're making a scene," Nadine agreed. "You need prayer something fierce! It's like you're possessed!"

The ride attendant released the bar that was holding them all in the moment the ride came to a halt. Without waiting for her passenger to exit first, Maude climbed over the poor woman and hightailed it off the platform.

"Well, I have never!" Nadine said.

"Oh, yes you have," Opal interrupted. "She's on a downward spiral. It's probably feeding time again."

"What?" Nadine asked. Even though she had known Opal since they were teenagers, she was still not one hundred percent used to the way that Opal spoke about things. "Wait for me!"

Nadine clambered after Opal who was chasing after Maude. By the time she found them, the group of nuns had already surrounded Maude to pray for her soul. Ruby and Opal had managed to shift their way out of the circle to the side.

"What in the world?" Nadine gasped. She was out of breath from having chased Opal through the crowd.

"Apparently Maude's behavior on the ride was a little less than holy," Ruby whispered. "They said she needed some prayers."

"That's one way to put it," Nadine said. "I've never heard such language."

After the circle broke apart and Maude apologized profusely, she joined Nadine, Ruby, and Opal at the nearby picnic table.

"That was so embarrassing," Ruby hissed.

"Who are you telling?" Maude huffed. She rounded on Nadine and snapped, "You shouted that I was possessed!"

"I have been saying for years that you need to get a handle on your temper," Opal said. "So many issues, so little time."

"Don't get me started again, Opal Tyler," Maude growled.

"Y'all hush!" Nadine chastised. She glanced at her watch and gasped. "Oh my goodness! I can't believe how late it is. I have to get back to the hotel to get ready. I'm going to see a show on Broadway tonight!"

"How fun!" Ruby exclaimed. "I wish we could have gotten tickets for a show while we were here."

"You know what, why don't we meet for lunch tomorrow and I'll tell you all about it! There's a wonderful Italian place called Nico's not far from our hotel. Why don't we meet in the lobby around noon and walk down there?" Nadine suggested.

"Sounds wonderful," Ruby smiled. Before Maude could protest, Ruby cut her a look that silenced her.

"Lovely!" Nadine gushed. "Ta ta for now. See you all tomorrow. And Maude, you still have food on your chin."

Maude wiped her chin off with the back of her sleeve while Ruby and Opal said their goodbyes.

"Well, I think it's about time we made our way back to the hotel ourselves," Ruby said. "I'm looking forward to a nice dinner at the hotel this evening and then getting some rest."

"Me too," Maude agreed. "How about we play some cards before bed?"

"Only if you don't cheat," Opal instructed.

"Oh hush. I can't help that you two are terrible at cards," Maude laughed.

"Only because I'm never quite certain what the rules for that game you like actually are," Ruby explained.

"Hand and foot is very complex," Maude nodded. She continued to explain the rules of the game the entire way back to the hotel.

"And you win, just like that," Maude continued. "It's simple really."

"I still don't get it," Ruby whispered to Opal.

Throughout dinner, Maude continued to try and explain the rules of the card game she had grown up playing. After they ordered their drinks and entrees, Opal struck up conversation with a nearby table on the price of stocks. Ruby and Maude easily tuned them out. After Ruby again admitted that the rules of the card game were too much for her to remember, Maude borrowed a pen from a passing waiter and began to scribble on the cloth napkin by her plate.

"Maude! No!" Ruby gasped. "You can't write on that. I am mortified!"

"You can use it as a reference!" Maude objected.

"They're going to kick us out of the Plaza!" Ruby said.

"Oh hush, I'll show you an example of the perfect hand," Maude said. She rifled through her purse that she had thrown underneath her chair.

"Maude Cooper! You did not bring those ratty cards to supper. Put them away!" Ruby hissed.

"The food is taking too long," Maude mumbled. "But fine!" She shoved the deck of cards back into her purse and frowned. "I wrote the rules down for you both to use."

Opal had sat back down in her seat and took the napkin from Maude. "You added quite a few new addendums," Opal mused. She turned the napkin over in her hands and squinted. "And this one is new, too. Jokers are wild in poker. And where in the world did this point system come from? You never were any good at math."

"I was, too!" Maude objected.

"Opal's right," Ruby agreed. She looked the napkin over and shook her head. "This whole section is new rules!"

"No it ain't!" Maude countered.

"Can't we play Go Fish or Old Maid instead," Ruby asked.

Opal collapsed into a fit of giggles. "Old Maid! She sure called you out, Maude. We could call it Old Maude instead," she chuckled.

Ruby smiled and covered her face with her clean napkin. They were saved by the introduction of their entrees. Maude agreed that the filet mignon was prepared perfectly, and Ruby's seared chicken breast was some of the fanciest chicken she had ever eaten. Opal ordered the scallops and asked for the chef's recipe because the sauce they were seared with was delicious.

They all managed to save room for the most decadent creme brûlée's that were otherworldly. By the time they got back upstairs to their room, they were all stuffed.

They quickly settled into their pajamas and Maude dealt the cards for the game.

"Ruby, do you need one last refresher on the ever-changing rules?" Opal laughed.

"I think I'll learn as I go," Ruby chuckled.

Maude rolled her eyes and threw the cloth napkin she had destroyed at Ruby.

~Chapter Sixteen~

"Don't forget we're meeting Nadine around noon," Ruby reminded them. She buttoned her purple shirt in the mirror and started to clean out her purse.

"How could I forget?" Maude sighed. "We could just go to Broadway ourselves instead of hearing about her night."

"I would like to walk down the street," Opal agreed. She blew on her freshly painted nails and lightly fanned them in front of her so they would dry quicker.

"I meant a Broadway show," Maude corrected.

"Ahh, that's where most people get confused," Opal explained. "Broadway is a street, not a particular theater or show. It's a bunch of theaters and shows all along the street."

"Well, I knew that," mumbled Maude.

"I'm sure you did," teased Opal.

"I'm sure we'll have time to meet Nadine for a quick lunch and then visit Broadway. It's our last evening here, so I definitely want to do as much as we can," Ruby said.

"We could have lunch with her any day of the week in Rhinestone. Not that I want to, but I don't know why we have to meet her again on vacation," Maude grumbled.

"Because we're being neighborly!" Ruby said. "Knock it off and let yourself have a good time. I think half the time y'all just feel the need to keep up appearances of your spat and it gets out of hand. Y'all will be fine for a while and then one of you gets the itch to bother the other one and it spirals! I swear!"

"Now you made Ruby swear," sighed Opal. "Geez Maude, you really can't help yourself, can you?"

Maude took a deep breath and nodded. "You're right, Ruby. I'm going to be the bigger person and have a nice lunch with my neighbor and your friend."

Opal chuckled quietly and Ruby smiled, clearly appeased and proud of Maude's sudden maturation.

"Thank you, Maude," Ruby smiled. "Now, let's get ready to head that way. We're going to meet her down in the lobby and walk that way together."

"My nails are dry," Opal nodded. "Sure you don't want me to paint yours before we go, Maude? I've got a nice little purple that will match the little baggies under your eyes."

"With that new mumbo jumbo stuff you've been experimenting with? God no!" Maude shook her head.

"Suit yourself," Opal shrugged. "It's part of my all-natural line. Not that you have ever been overly concerned with what you put in and on your body."

"Y'all hush," Ruby sighed. "Now come on. We're already running late."

Nadine was already waiting for them down in the lobby wearing a tight pink dress, high heels, and a matching pink handbag. She looked like she stepped right out of a magazine.

"Oh! Should we have dressed up?" exclaimed Ruby. She looked at Maude who was wearing denim jeans and a t-shirt. "Should we go change?"

"Of course not," Nadine assured her. "I'm going to Tiffany's after lunch, so I wanted to look my best. You look fine, Ruby. And Opal, you always look amazing."

Opal smiled radiantly in her black capris, floral patterned shirt, and matching headband.

Ruby frowned slightly, but recovered quickly. "Ok, if you're sure."

"Nico's isn't fancy at all. Y'all will fit right on in," Nadine smiled.

"She won't," Maude snickered.

"What was that, Maude?" Nadine asked.

"Oh, nothing," Maude shrugged. "We ready to go?"

Nadine smiled and led the way out of the front doors. Nico's was just a few blocks away, and even though she was wearing high heels, she didn't miss a beat.

When they walked up to the restaurant doors, Maude knew immediately that Nadine would stick out like a sore thumb. This was the epitome of what one would call a hole-in-the-wall. Nadine held the door open and ushered them inside.

"How did you find this place?" Maude asked her.

"Oh, I saw a lovely little flier at one of the coffee shops I went to and knew this would be the perfect place!" Nadine grinned.

The inside of the restaurant was dingy and the lights were dim. There were tables of all shapes and sizes haphazardly scattered around the floor, and none of the chairs matched. Ruby's shoes squeaked when she walked across the floor.

"You here for the cannoli contest?" a gruff voice asked.

"The what?" Ruby asked.

"Oh, didn't I tell you?" Nadine smiled mischievously.

"Tell us what?" Maude asked.

"Must have slipped my mind," Nadine shrugged. "Oh well, we're here now!"

She waltzed over to the man behind the counter. He handed her a clipboard and she furiously wrote something on it. "Alright, that should do it."

"It starts in fifteen minutes," the man huffed. "Take a seat."

"Oh, no, I'm not doing that," Nadine cackled. "Not in this dress."

"Then why'd you sign up?" he demanded.

Nadine read his name tag on his apron before smiling. "Oh, Mario, My lovely friend, Maude, is going to compete," Nadine smiled.

"Which one of you is Maude?" Mario wondered.

Nadine, Opal, and Ruby all looked over at Maude who was still positioned in the doorway.

251

"Will someone tell me what's going on?" Maude demanded.

"Must be her," he growled. He looked over his shoulder at two hulking men who wore sauced stained aprons. "Think this broad can do it?"

"Did he just call me a broad?" Maude muttered.

"That's only because he doesn't know you yet," Opal assured her.

"Not a chance," the first one laughed.

"Nah," the second agreed. "No one can beat Joey."

"First of all, don't call me a broad. And second, who the hell is Joey?" Maude demanded.

"I'm Joey," a voice croaked from the corner booth. All of their heads snapped towards where the voice was from. "I've won this competition five years in a row." He jerked his finger towards the cash register and pointed to the five framed photographs tacked to the wall above it. "I'm unbeatable."

"Says who?" Maude asked. She stood up tall and puffed out her chest.

"Says me," Joey laughed.

Maude scowled and looked at Nadine. "What in the world have you got me into?"

"You can bow out," Nadine offered. "It's ok to quit. Nothing wrong with admitting that someone else got the best of you."

Before Maude could offer a rebuttal, Opal stood up on her chair and shouted, "Maude's going to eat more cannolis than you ever have."

The men laughed at her and looked around at each other, but Opal wasn't going to be outdone that easily. "She's going to beat you so bad that you'll go crying home to your mamas! But don't worry, I've got some all-natural laxatives that will take care of any stomach aches you get."

"Opal!" Maude said. She had been on the receiving end of one of those homemade laxatives and she wouldn't wish that on anyone.

"But you don't know how many he can eat!" Ruby shrieked. She tugged at Opal's sleeve to get her attention and pull her back down to earth.

Opal pondered that for a moment. She wrinkled up her nose and said, "Maude will best your record, times two!"

"Opal!" Ruby gasped. "What are you doing?"

Joey and the men roared with laughter. "Well see," Joey howled. "My record's sixteen in three minutes."

Maude scrunched up her nose and frowned. "I can't eat thirty! Not in three minutes!" she scowled at Opal.

"Well, actually that would be thirty-two, but who's counting," Nadine cringed.

"You just have to eat seventeen," Ruby said. "Or more if he beats that. But just one more!"

"Opal said double!" Maude frowned.

"But Opal doesn't make the rules," Ruby reminded her.

"Oh, right," nodded Maude. She turned towards Joey and cleared her throat. "Is it just me and you?"

"No," Joey laughed. "Hey Rocco, Marty, Dean! You ready?"

Three hulking men appeared out of nowhere and crossed their arms.

"Alright, enough talkin,' let's get this started!," the man behind the counter said. "Let's get this started."

He ushered the four men and Maude to a long table covered with butcher paper. The kitchen staff brought out five heaping bowls full of cannolis and set them in front of each contender.

"Ok, you get three minutes to eat as much cannolis as you can. Don't worry," he looked at Maude. "No one's bettin' on you."

"Says who?" Ruby asked.

"I am," Opal said.

"So am I," Ruby nodded.

"Me too," frowned Nadine, which caused Maude to look at her with confusion.

"No one bets against a woman from Rhinestone," Nadine continued. The men's arrogant attitude had rubbed her the wrong way.

"Nadine rooting for me is almost scarier than this mound of cannolis," Maude mumbled.

"Don't be silly, Maude. Show them how it's done," Nadine encouraged. "If anyone can eat like a pig, it's you."

"There she is. That's the Nadine I know and tolerate," Maude said.

The gruff man ignored the women and continued with his spiel. "This here's my family recipe for cannolis. Joey's record is sixteen, so we got a dozen in each bowl. We can put less in yours if you like," he turned and grinned at Maude.

Maude cut her eyes at him and tucked the paper napkin into her shirt.

"You got three minutes to eat as much as you can. But it's gotta be the whole cannoli or it don't count.

And no barfing. I ain't cleanin' that mess up. We're a respectable place," Mario explained.

"Now, Ray's gonna watch the timer and count down for you all. Everyone ready?" he asked.

"Don't make yourself sick sweetheart!" Joey laughed.

"Did he just call me sweetheart?" Maude looked at Ruby.

"I wouldn't have done that," Opal shook her head.

"She's going to destroy these guys," Nadine said.

"You got this, Maude. Make us proud," Ruby said.

"Good luck," Joey laughed. "You're going to need it."

"Same to you," Maude said seriously.

Little did these men know that they were in the presence of a woman who took eating, and winning, very seriously. They were about to find out. As the countdown buzzer sounded, Maude wasted no time in grabbing her bowl and pulled it closer. She dug in with wild ferocity that no one was quite prepared for.

"She's not even chewing them!" Nadine gasped.

"I don't think that was one of the rules," Opal added.

"This is enough to make anyone sick," Nadine swallowed hard. She looked over at Ruby who also looked a little green. "Is she ok?"

"This is normal," Ruby assured her. "Maude's not going to ever bow out of any competition, let alone one that revolves around sweets."

"I once saw her enter a barbecue contest where she ate half the hog herself," Opal lamented.

Nadine looked at Ruby with wide eyes to see if Opal was telling the truth.

"It's true," Ruby nodded. "She's banned from Hank's Real Pit BBQ over in Junction because she, well, that's a story for another time."

Joey looked over at Maude with concern. He was halfway through his seventh cannoli while she had already inhaled half a dozen herself. He grabbed two and shoved them into his mouth. To his left, he noticed the other contestants were eyeing Maude with fear as well. She certainly didn't eat like any woman they had met before.

"Come on Maude, you've got him!" Nadine yelled.

Joey looked up at Nadine, Ruby, and Opal. Maude continued to devour the cannolis in the bowl in front of her as they cheered her on.

"She's going to beat him!" Ruby yelled.

Sure enough, Maude was staring at the bottom of her bowl. Joey had one left in his bowl.

The other three challengers were of no concern. They had long since dropped out from nausea and pure fascination from watching Joey and Maude go head-to-head. Maude was a good twenty or so years older than Joey, but that hadn't stopped her from matching his progress.

"Thirty seconds left," Ray called out.

Maude reached over and shoved the empty bowl into the lap of the nearest challenger who had surrendered. Opal pushed a full bowl of a dozen cannolis closer to her, and she began shoveling whole cannolis into her mouth with both hands. Joey swallowed his final pastry and pushed the empty bowl off the table. It clanged onto the floor with a loud shudder. He then grabbed another bowl with a dozen cannolis in them towards him.

"He's catching up!" Ruby squealed.

It was almost too much to watch for Nadine and Ruby. Opal, on the other hand, was riveted. She was the perfect hype girl to have on your side, and she knew how to use her powers in any situation.

"Is it me, or is it hot in here?" she stood up and fanned herself. Before their very eyes, she started to unbutton the top button on her shirt. Joey forgot about the cannoli in each hand and stared.

"Oh my lord!" Ruby yelled. "Opal Tyler! What in the world are you doing?"

"Go with me on this, Ruby. Trust me!" Opal winked.

Ruby's eyes widened and she shook her head. "I certainly will not!" she howled. She had certainly not woken up this morning expecting to witness a half-naked cannoli eating contest. When Nadine nodded at Opal and lifted her leg onto the chair and began to raise her tight pink dress, Joey dropped his cannolis on the floor.

"Party foul!" Opal yelled. "Automatic disqualification!"

"You don't make the rules!" Ruby and Mario both shrieked.

Maude wasn't paying Opal and Nadine any attention. She was too focused on finishing the rest of the cannolis in the bowl. She didn't look over at Joey who had all but stopped eating by this point.

"Time!" Mario yelled. He slammed the timer onto the table and looked at Maude who belched loudly.

"Always the lady," Nadine said with a grimace.

"You're one to talk," Ruby said. "My heaven's! What in the world has gotten into y'all!"

"I can't believe it," Mario said. "We have a new champion. She ate twenty cannolis."

"Twenty?" Joey howled. He hiccupped loudly and beckoned for Ray to bring him a glass of water.

Maude looked a little green around the gills as Ruby, Opal, and Nadine all began to pat her on her back. She quickly held her hand to her mouth. She didn't trust her stomach not to rebel against her.

"Twenty?" Joey shouted again. "But they cheated!"

"Says who?" Maude grumbled.

Joey looked dumbfounded. "They practically took their clothes off!" he shouted.

"We did no such thing," Nadine gasped. "You mind your manners."

"We didn't stop you from eating. We merely provided some entertainment," Opal said.

Mario shook his head. "I guess there's nothing in the rules about fan support."

"Fan support?" Joey shrieked. "Fan support? My fans don't behave like that!"

"What fans?" Opal asked.

"Maybe they don't like you as much as my friends like me," Maude said.

"This is ridiculous!" Joey fumed. He picked up his jacket and stormed out of the restaurant.

"That was amazing Maude!" Nadine said. "You really showed them."

"Here's your prize," Mario said. He handed her a wrinkled white t-shirt and a plastic box with a half dozen cannolis inside.

"Thanks," Maude sighed. She took the box and shirt and shoved them into her purse.

"Alright, I'm hungry. Maude, since you're the big winner, you pick where we eat," Opal announced.

Ruby winced at Maude's grimace. All Nadine could do was laugh.

❧ Chapter Seventeen ❧

"Bye Nadine!" Ruby called after her.

Nadine smiled and waved goodbye before stepping into her waiting taxi.

"So nice to have a good southern lunch with a neighbor from home," Ruby said.

"I have to admit, that wasn't so bad after all," Maude said. She patted her bulging stomach and let out a loud burp.

"Have you ever met a hamburger you didn't like?" Opal questioned.

"I meant having lunch with Nadine," Maude rolled her eyes. "But if either of you ever tell her that, I'll lie."

"I'm glad to see you're back on the upswing of things with her," Ruby nodded.

"What does that mean?" Maude asked.

"Like I said before. You two always go round and round. One minute you're fine with each other and then the next minute you're back trying to make each other's lives miserable!" Ruby explained.

"I wouldn't say that we're fine with each other," Maude corrected.

"You know what I mean," eyed Ruby.

"And I wouldn't say we make each other's lives ruined or miserable per se," Maude continued. "She'll always be a thorn in my side though."

"You really are impossible," Ruby sighed. She continued to thumb through her New York City guidebook and frowned. "I wish we had one more day. There's still so much we haven't done."

"Tell that to my legs," laughed Maude. "I think we've walked across the city and back five times by now."

"There's so much to do here," Ruby said again.

"We'll just have to come back again soon," Opal announced. "Alright, now that Maude's finished with her after lunch ice cream, let's head over to Wall Street. You know I love a man in a suit!"

"I'm surprised that yall didn't wanna go with Nadine over to that Tiffany place," Maude said as she stretched.

"That Tiffany place?" Opal echoed.

"Maude! That Tiffany place is the epitome of elegance," Ruby gasped.

Maude shrugged and shook remnants of the ice cream cone off her sweatshirt. "I'm just saying that I'm surprised y'all didn't want to go. The way y'all all talked about it like y'all were gaga over some jewelry."

"It's luxurious jewelry," Ruby corrected. "It's not your everyday run-of-the-mill kind of place. It definitely is a once in a lifetime opportunity, but I don't need to buy anything from there. Jameson would kill me," she laughed.

"I think I'll stick with my opal from Wilbur," Opal smiled. "I was thinking of having it made into a pendant for a necklace. Wilbur is so sweet and so clever to find them! There's no telling what all is hidden in that forest."

"A necklace would be so pretty!" Ruby cooed. "I think I want to do that, too. We can all have matching ones!"

Maude nodded and smiled at the idea. "I'd much rather wear a necklace than a ring any old day."

"Then it's settled," Opal smiled.

"Hearing y'all talk about that place though, I just don't get it. Who would spend that much money on something that you could just lose. Nadine talking about buying herself matching earrings to go with her necklace. And then another tiara? All I've heard about since the day she won was that blasted tiara from school. Now she's going to go and get herself another one," Maude huffed.

"We can swing by there ourselves if you really want one," teased Ruby.

Maude stuck her tongue out at her as Opal laughed. "Maude doesn't have the head shape for a tiara. Her head is too boxy."

"I'll show you boxy!" Maude retorted. She popped Opal on the behind with her box of cannolis that she hadn't yet opened. Even though she was able to eat a deluxe cheeseburger, French fries, and an ice cream for lunch, she wasn't sure that she would be able to eat another cannoli for quite some time. That eating competition had done her in when it came to the Italian pastry.

They gathered up their things and followed the map in Ruby's guidebook towards Wall Street. Like every place in New York, it was fairly crowded. They were in awe of the New York Stock Exchange building on the corner of Wall Street and Broad Street. It was some of the most beautiful architecture that they had seen.

"What is there to do here?" Maude asked after Ruby had taken what felt like hundreds of pictures of the building and people walking by.

"We can go see Trinity Church if you like," Opal offered.

"What's that?" Maude asked.

"Seriously Maude, don't you ever read? Or do your research before we go anywhere?" Opal gasped.

"No," Maude replied. "I never have to because you two bookworms do it enough for all of us."

"To answer your question," Ruby interjected. She flipped through the guidebook and read aloud. "Trinity Church was originally built in 1848, making it one of the oldest churches in the city. It is home to many notable New Yorkers, including the one and only Alexander Hamilton."

"I think I remember that name," Maude nodded.

"Heaven help us," Ruby sighed.

"He was one of the founding fathers," Opal nudged her and blinked rapidly. "Remember?"

"No, I don't think he was a president," Maude argued.

"I didn't say he was a President. He said he was one of the founding fathers," Opal repeated.

"Same thing," Maude smirked.

"Not the same thing at all," Ruby huffed. "Come on! You've got a lot of history to learn and it's only a short walk to get there."

Opal and Maude followed behind Ruby as she read page after page of the guidebook, interspersed with her own knowledge and historical trivia facts. By the time they arrived at the beautiful building, Maude was well caught up with history thanks to Ruby. They stood in awe of the stained-glass windows and marveled at the rows of headstones that revealed famous historical names.

"I always get creeped out looking at graves," Maude whispered.

"Aren't they fascinating!" Opal mused. "Just think, the great minds of America are mere feet from us! Like you could reach down and touch them! Or they could reach up."

"Shh, y'all don't talk like that," Ruby whispered back. "It feels shameful to talk about the dead like that."

"They can't hear us," Maude shrugged.

"They can hear you," Opal said seriously.

Maude pulled her hands inside her sweatshirt and looked around. "Ok, are we done here? This is getting creepier by the minute."

"Let's walk towards Broadway and do some yoga stretches in front of the theatres," Opal suggested. "Just being in that area gives me a new zest for life!"

"I ain't doing any kind of yoga stretches in front of anyone," Maude whispered to Ruby.

"I heard that," Opal said. "And so did they!" She flung out her arms and pretended to fly out of the cemetery gates back towards the street.

"A new zest for life," mumbled Maude. "She ain't ever lost the old zesty one."

Broadway was full of people walking in all directions. People of all ages and in all types of clothing were taking photographs of the brilliant signs on the theatres.

"Look! Barry Manilow is coming to town!" Maude said. "I love him!" She started to sing an offkey version of his greatest hits.

"Take a picture of that, Ruby," Opal laughed. "You won't do yoga with me, but you'll do whatever that dance is called."

"Barry brings out the best in me," Maude said.

"I'll keep that in mind," Ruby laughed.

They took more photographs and walked down the busy street to read the marquees that revealed the names of the shows each theatre was hosting. Besides Barry Manilow, none stuck out to them, which made them feel better about not being able to get tickets to any show during their visit.

"Before we head back to the hotel, let's do a little more shopping," suggested Ruby.

They perused the different street vendors and popped into the different side shops along the way. Before long, they were all carrying a shopping bag full of printed shirts and eclectic souvenirs.

"Look over there!" Opal squealed. She pointed across the street to a table with canvas prints stacked across it. A man sat behind a canvas painting a young couple as they posed.

They hurried across the street and watched as the man sat behind the canvas. He didn't have any paints or brushes nearby, but instead had a box of large markers and pencils. "Oh! He's drawing them! I can't wait to see what it looks like!" Ruby said. "Maybe we can sit for our portrait next!"

The man nodded and pointed to a clipboard next to him. Ruby signed her name and reviewed the price list. "We'll do the bigger one," she nodded. "Since there's three of us to squeeze in."

A few minutes later, the artist smiled and turned the portrait around to face the couple. Opal burst into giggles and Ruby clamped her hand over her mouth.

"What is that?" Maude asked.

"It's a caricature!" laughed Opal. "We are definitely getting this done!"

"A what?" Ruby asked.

"A caricature portrait," Opal explained. "It's a picture where the artist exaggerates features. I can't wait to see how he draws us!"

"I don't know about this, Opal," Ruby frowned.

"Oh, come on," Maude agreed. "It can't be that bad. We're all near perfect! Maybe it'll just look regular for us."

After the couple paid, the artist handed the portrait to the couple and they gleefully went on their way. "Ok, sit here," he instructed Ruby and Opal to sit in the chairs in front of his easel. "And you stand behind," he said to Maude.

They did as they were told and tried to stay as still as possible. Every time the man smiled or frowned, Ruby couldn't help but wince. "I have a bad feeling about this," she whispered.

"It's going to be great!" Opal whispered back.

After a few more minutes of waiting, the artist announced that he was finished. "What do you think!" he said as he turned the portrait around to face them.

"Wow!" exclaimed Opal.

"Oh my!" Ruby gasped.

"You've got to be kidding me!" Maude grunted.

The artist took Ruby's camera and snapped a picture of the three of them with their new portrait. "It's good," he nodded. He placed the drawing in a clear bag and handed it to Opal while Ruby paid.

"Well, he certainly thought a lot of you," Maude said loudly to Opal. "Dolly Parton called and wants her cleavage back."

"You're just mad because he made your nose so big," Opal laughed.

Maude rubbed her nose and grimaced.

"He clearly focused on our best and brightest features," Opal continued.

"Did he have to make my eyes look like tea saucers?" Ruby whispered. "They're huge!"

"I love it!" exclaimed Opal. "We've never looked better!" She hugged the bag containing the drawing close to her chest.

"Then you can keep it at your house," Ruby offered.

"I'll keep it first! Then we can rotate it,"
Opal agreed.

"You can have my turn," Ruby and Maude both said at the same time.

"I know just where I'm going to put it," Opal grinned. Maude and Ruby were both too scared to ask.

When they got back to the hotel, Opal began to show everyone in the lobby and in the line for the elevators their portrait. Ruby and Maude covered their faces and stood a ways back from her to distance themselves.

"Did you have to show half the hotel that thing?" Maude asked once they were back in their room upstairs.

"Everyone loved it!" Opal smiled.

"I'm sure they did," Maude rolled her eyes. "I don't want to pack up. It's strange, I'm ready to get back home to Rhinestone, but I really have enjoyed this trip."

Ruby nodded and folded the new shirts she had bought. "I don't know if we're going to be able to bring all this back. We may need to get another set of luggage," she said. "I need a separate bag for all of my dirty laundry."

"You can put some of your stuff in my yellow suitcase over there," Opal offered. "I always pack light."

It didn't take them long to pack, even though they had accumulated quite a bit of new things during their adventures.

"It's our last night in the Big Apple," Opal said as she looked out of the window. "Where should we eat dinner? What should we do?"

"The world is our oyster. That's what the saying is, right?" Ruby asked.

"Yes ma'am!" Opal smiled.

Maude bit her nail and thought hard. "What about we go to a comedy club?"

"I love to laugh!" Ruby said. "Where is the comedy club at?" She grabbed her guide book and looked through the pages. "I don't see one listed here."

"I don't know," Maude shrugged. "We can ask someone downstairs. Let me change clothes really quick."

As soon as they were all ready, they descended to the lobby in the elevator. Opal walked over to one of the valets and shamelessly began to flirt. A few minutes later, she skipped back over to Maude and Ruby with an address.

The taxi dropped them off in front of a bustling nightclub with a line wrapped around the building a few minutes later.

"We're never going to get in!" Ruby fretted.

"Oh yes we will," Maude said. "Opal, go work your magic!" She shoved Opal towards the men wearing black suits at the head of the line. As predicted, it didn't take long for her to usher Maude and Ruby over.

"I don't know how she does it!" Ruby whispered to Maude.

"Who cares! Probably best not to know," Maude whispered back. "Let's go!"

They were led to three seats five rows back from the stage. A single microphone stood in the center of the stage.

"I wonder who will be onstage?" Maude set once they were settled in their seats. "I didn't see any signs outside."

"Maybe it's an open mic night," Opal said.

"I hope not!" Maude said. "I can just imagine the jokes you'd get up there and tell."

Opal and Ruby grinned.

They didn't have to wait long before a man wearing khaki pants, a blue button-down shirt, and a white bowtie walked onto the stage behind the microphone. "Good evening ladies and gentlemen! We've got seven different comics here tonight to wow you with their humor. The funniest one will move on to our second-round next week. Now please put your hands together for our first comic of the night, Tim Michaelson."

A short man wearing a sweater vest walked onstage and took the microphone. "Hello, hello. They say I've got about ten minutes before I have to pass the mic, so let's get started," he said jovially.

He was funny enough, but the crowd wasn't sad when he passed the mic off to the next performer. As the night wore on, the comics steadily got funnier. The last comic was the best of the night. He was a perfect blend of sass and self-deprecating humor. There was no doubt in anyone's mind that he should be the one to move on to the next round.

"That was a great idea," Opal said to Maude once they were back on the street. "Let's go eat supper at Ellen's Stardust Diner."

"As long as they've got food, I don't care where we go," Maude said.

"I read about that place!" Ruby blurted out. "It's a retro 1950s themed restaurant near Broadway! It's the best restaurant in the city! They sing and dance and I'm sure it's simply magical!"

"Who sings and dances?" Maude asked.

"The servers do! They're actors and actresses on Broadway! This is their other job," Ruby exclaimed. "What's RE we waiting for! Let's go!"

∽Chapter Eighteen∽

"Rise and shine!" Opal called out. She flung open the curtains and then ripped the covers off of a sleeping Maude. "It's our final morning in New York City! Wake up!"

Ruby was already brushing her hair in the mirror by the bathroom "This trip has just flown by! Hurry up, Maude. We have just enough time to go eat a quick breakfast before coming back here to get our luggage."

"Ok," Maude yawned. She got ready in record time and stretched her arms over her head. Ruby winced at the noises of Maude's bones popping.

"That doesn't seem healthy," Opal added.

Maude rolled her eyes at Opal and pulled on her tennis shoes.

"Ellen's was so good last night! I'm glad we decided to go back for breakfast this morning. Why didn't we find that place earlier?" Ruby said.

The taxi ride over to the diner didn't take long. Even though there was a long line to be seated, it moved quickly. They already knew exactly what they wanted to order.

Opal chose waffles, while Ruby ordered a stack of pancakes. Maude couldn't decide between the pancakes or waffles, so she got a short stack of both with extra bacon. The atmosphere was just as magical as it had been the night before. They didn't want to leave, but time was ticking closer to their flight and they still had to get back to the hotel to get their luggage.

As Maude started to cut into the last of her pancakes, Opal suddenly stood up and squealed with delight.

"Hello Uncle Frankie!" Opal shouted with a wave across the restaurant.

Maude was too busy spreading butter on her pancakes to look up. She was used to Opal's random outburst. She only stopped to pay attention because Ruby began nervously slapping her hand.

"Ruby! What on earth is the matter with you?" she asked with a huff.

Ruby was staring open mouthed at Opal and the man she was hugging enthusiastically around the neck.

"Hiya, doll face," the man said to Opal.

"Oh my God! Is that?" Maude asked, now staring in equal disbelief with Ruby.

"Yes," Ruby muttered. "Yes, it is."

"Why didn't you tell me you were in town? We coulda had lunch?" Uncle Frank said to Opal.

"Last I heard you were on the west coast. I didn't realize you were back," Opal explained. "Silly me!"

"Just got back. You know I'm a New Yorker at heart," he smiled.

"What a shame!" Opal said. "Maybe you can join us for breakfast before we fly out."

Uncle Frank looked over at the table where Maude and Ruby sat in stunned silence. "Hiya, ladies," he nodded. "I'd love to, but I'm on my way to a meeting with my producer."

"Next time then," Opal smiled.

"It's a date, doll," Uncle Frankie said. He hugged Opal tightly once again before turning toward the door.

As he passed the table, he smiled at Ruby and Maude. "Ladies."

Ruby and Maude watched him walk out the door with their jaws on the floor. They had not noticed that Opal had sat back down and was drinking the glass of water.

"Was that?" Maude stammered. "No. It can't be."

Ruby nodded slowly. "Yes," she whispered. "Yes, it was."

"How?" Maude mumbled, this time turning her attention to Opal.

"Would you pass the butter?" Opal asked Maude.

Maude stared at Opal before turning her attention to Ruby who was looking as perplexed as she felt. "Pass the butter?" she snapped her head back to Opal. "You're just going to sit there and ask for butter like nothing happened?"

"What?" Opal asked innocently. "I just want a little for this last half of the waffle. I'll save the rest for you."

"Opal! Uncle Frankie," Ruby said. "What in the world?"

"Oh! It was really good to see him. I wish I'd known he was in town," Opal said. "His lunch parties are the best."

"His lunch parties?" Maude asked.

"Opal! Explain yourself!" Ruby demanded. "How in the world do you know him?"

"Uncle Frankie?" Opal asked.

"Of course, Uncle Frankie!" Maude said. "Who else would we be talking about?"

"Oh I've known him for years. Aunt Willie and him have been friends for ages. He always said she had the best laugh," Opal said, taking a bite of her waffle. "But he says I have the best smile. He's such a sweetheart."

"He and old aunt Willie were friends?" Ruby asked.

Opal nodded. "Oh yeah. They've known each other for years. She used to go out west and visit him, and of course whenever he's in the area he stops by Junction to get some of her famous canned okra and jars of muscadine jam."

Ruby and Maude stared at each other. This was simply too much to take in.

Opal added some more butter to her waffle and continued as if nothing unusual was happening. "And he was so supportive when I started Color Me Crazy. He loves the shampoo and conditioner. Says his hair has never been so soft. I really should have asked him when he'll need his next shipment so I can box some up for him."

Ruby shook her head trying to find the voice to ask all the questions running around her head, but Maude beat her to it.

"Wait just a minute!" Maude began. "Are you sitting here telling us that Frank Sinatra knows your aunt and has visited the Rhinestone area?"

"Of course that's what I'm telling you. Haven't you been listening?" Opal shook her head. "Honestly, Maude, I really think you need to get your hearing checked. Between your bones cracking and your nose growing longer, I think we might have to put you down."

"Opal, we've known each other since we played together in the sandbox. How is it that we didn't know about this?" Ruby asked.

Opal thought for a moment. "I'm sure I mentioned my Uncle Frank before. In fact, I know I have!"

"I don't remember you ever saying anything about an uncle Frankie, and you dang sure haven't mentioned Frank Sinatra!" Maude was outdone.

Opal shrugged. "I certainly have. When we were in Nepal I told the hotel staff about him. Remember?"

"Oh my Lord, she did!" gasped Ruby. She grabbed her napkin and covered her mouth with it. "Maude! Remember?"

Maude's eyes grew as wide as saucers. "I thought she was kidding! So did you!"

"Why would I kid about something as silly as that? As soon as we got back to Rhinestone, I wrote him a letter telling him all about our adventures. He sent the hotel an autographed photo and everything for taking care of us," Opal smiled.

"Well I'll be damned," Maude fumbled. "And he comes to Rhinestone? To visit you?"

"When he gets the chance," Opal nodded. "He is a very busy man. He hasn't stopped by in years and years. Usually I took aunt Willy over to Junction to see him, but it's been so long. He lets me know when he needs some product and I shop it over to him. He's one of my best clients."

Maude crossed her arms and looked from one to the other. "I've never seen him in Junction or heard tale of him being there!"

"I guess you don't know where to look," Opal shrugged.

"I guess I don't either," Ruby mumbled. "Opal Tyler, you are full of surprises! I'll be!"

Opal smiled and looked at her watch. "Oh goodness, we better get back to the hotel and get our things. Our flight leaves in three hours."

"Oh goodness!" Ruby exclaimed. Once Maude was finished and the bill was paid, they hurried to call a taxi to take them back to the hotel to get their luggage that was thankfully already packed and ready to go.

Opal asked the taxi driver to stay put while they ran upstairs to get their suitcases. While she checked out in the hotel lobby, Ruby and Maude figured out how to get all of their luggage into the cab. It was a tight fit, but they made it to the airport in record time.

"I need a nap," Maude announced. "It's already been such a busy morning."

"You can nap on the plane," Ruby suggested.

"You know I don't like to sleep on the plane. Flying makes me nervous," Maude sighed.

"Let's get some coffee," Opal offered. She led them to a small coffee stand near their gate and ordered three cups of coffee. When Ruby and Maude weren't looking, she turned her back to them at the counter and poured a teaspoon sized amount of dark amber liquid into Maude's cup. She hurried over to where Maude and Ruby were sitting and sat down in the empty seat at the table.

"This is pretty good," Opal smiled. "Drink up."

Maude drank quickly, hoping the coffee would help her stay awake on the flight to Atlanta. Thankfully, this flight was a direct flight to Atlanta and didn't require any stops on the way home. After a few minutes of small talk, Ruby looked at her watch and said they needed to start boarding soon.

Maude yawned and threw away her empty coffee cup. She gathered up her purse and yawned again. "You sure you didn't give me decaf by mistake?" she asked Opal.

"No ma'am," Opal assured her. "I know your lifelong motto has always been that decaf coffee belongs in the trash can."

"Exactly," Maude agreed. "There's no point in decaf coffee."

"Right," Opal winked at Ruby.

"What did you do?" Ruby whispered.

Opal ignored Ruby's question and let the way towards the gate. They got in line to board and found three seats next to each other.

"Don't see any nuns," Maude said loudly. "Should be safe." She yawned again and shook her head. "I'm so tired. I feel like I could sleep for a hundred years!"

Opal grinned and sat down in her seat next to the window. She opened a package of gum and offered a piece to Ruby and Maude who both took some. "It helps with the ear popping," Opal reminded them.

Ruby sat down in the seat and eyed Opal warily. Maude sat down in the empty seat between Ruby and the aisle and closed her eyes.

"Opal, what did you do?" Ruby whispered to Opal again.

"Nothing, Ruby," Opal smiled. "I'm just helping her relax and take a little nap."

"You didn't! Opal! You drugged her!" Ruby shrieked.

"It's all natural," Opal said. "Keep your voice down or everyone will want some!"

"Well, I certainly don't!" Ruby sniffed.

"It's fine, Ruby. She'll take a little nap and be fine as wine when we land," Opal smiled.

Ruby shook her head at Opal and glanced over at Maude who was now loudly snoring. People stared at her as they walked down the aisle to get to their seats. When the plane took off twenty minutes later, Ruby was sure that she would wake up, but she did not. Maude's snoring went on uninterrupted for the entire flight back down south.

"Should we wake her up?" Ruby asked Opal. "We should be landing any minute."

Opal nodded and reached across Ruby's lap. She shook Maude's arm, but Maude kept snoring. Opal shrugged and muttered, "guess she's extra tired."

"What's re we going to do?" Ruby yelped. "She has to wake up! We can't leave her on the plane."

"We'll drag her behind us," Opal said matter of factly. "You know good and darn well this isn't the first time we've had to drag Maude out of somewhere."

"This is embarrassing! Everybody's been staring at us for the past few hours," Ruby grimaced.

"They haven't been staring at us. They've been staring at Maude. They probably feel sorry for us, or envious of her. That's some food solid sleep right there. She has quite the talent for snoring. I don't reckon she's taken very many breaths," Opal said.

Maude snorted and went silent for three seconds before breaking the sound waves again.

"This is madness!" Ruby cried. She shook Maude's shoulder a little harder than she intended to, and grabbed her head to keep it from rolling. "Wake up! Nap time is over!"

"What in tarnation are you doing?" Maude wailed. "Help! She's trying to kill me!"

"Stop it!" Ruby hissed. "You're making another scene. Hush!"

Maude rubbed her eyes and looked around drunkenly. "Ruby? Is that you? Why were you trying to choke me?"

"I wasn't choking you!" Ruby hissed. "But it's time to wake up. It's almost time."

"Almost time for takeoff?" Maude yawned. "I must have dozed off for a few minutes."

"Time to land," Ruby finished.

"Land?" Maude snapped to attention. "What do you mean land?"

"You've been sawing logs this entire time," Opal stated. "I can't say that's it's been pleasurable for the rest of us onboard, but you should feel well rested."

Maude looked around at the other passengers who were still staring at her. She looked at her watch in disbelief. "What? Snoring? I was just resting my eyes for a few minutes."

"Resting your eyes and wrecking our eardrums," chimed Opal.

Maude leaned over Ruby and Opal to look out of the window. Sure enough, they were getting lower and lower in the sky. "We are seriously about to land?" she asked.

Opal and Ruby both nodded.

"I guess I was pretty tired to miss takeoff and everything," Maude mused.

"Oh yes," Opal agreed. She patted Maude's hand and then gasped. "Um, Maude, what did you do with that gum that I gave you?"

Maude shrugged and thought for a second. "Must have swallowed it, I guess."

"That's nice," Opal murmured. She shook her head slightly at Ruby who was interrupted by the intercom announcing that they were about to land in Atlanta.

Maude braced her knuckles on the armrest and began her deep breathing exercises. She closed her eyes, leaned forward to put her head between her knees, and started to count to one hundred in a whisper.

After she made sure that Maude wasn't looking, Opal jerked her head at Ruby and whispered, "gum in hair."

"What?" Ruby gasped. She felt around her hair in a panic. "I still have mine."

"Not you," Opal said. "I repeat, gum in hair." She jerked her finger at Maude.

Ruby's eyes widened in shock. There was a fried wad of gum glued into the back of Maude's head. They weren't sure how it had gotten all the way back there, but it wasn't coming out easily.

"We'll have to deal with that later," Ruby sighed.

"I know a good salon," Opal said seriously. "To be fair, she has needed a good cut for months."

The plane landed with a few bumps and braked to a stop. Maude leaned back in her seat and took a deep breath. "That was too terrible. All in all, it was probably the easiest flight I've ever been on."

~Chapter Nineteen~

Maude found it a little difficult to walk a straight line. She held onto Ruby as they walked off the plane. She had felt this way before, after a night out on the town drinking. Only this time she didn't have any aches or pains, nor did she have any nausea. She felt like she had slept for three days straight and needed some more time to acclimate back to life.

Once they had obtained their baggage from baggage claim, she sat down on a nearby bench and rubbed her eyes. She then yawned loudly and announced that she would probably need another cup of coffee before she could drive them back to Rhinestone.

"There's no way you're driving us home. Not in this condition," Ruby half shouted.

"What do you mean by this condition?" Maude asked. "I'm just a little tired is all. Another coffee will do the trick."

Opal rummaged in her bag and found a small purple vial. "Yes, let's get another round of coffees for the road."

"No!" Ruby yelled. "No more coffees, and no more of your secret voodoo, Opal Tyler."

"This is a reversal dose," Opal explained. "An antidote, if you will."

"A what?" Maude gasped. "What is going on?"

"Let's get you that coffee," Opal smiled.

"Wait a minute," Maude said. "What's going on here?"

"Opal drugged you!" Ruby blurted out. "That's why you slept the whole time while the rest of us had to listen to your truck engine noises."

"What?" Maude roared.

"It's not a drug, Ruby. It's an all-natural sleep aid. And it works quite well, thank you very much!" Opal rebutted.

"Do you have something in that magic bag to get gum out of one's hair?" Ruby asked sarcastically.

"As a matter of fact, yes, I do," Opal smiled.

"Gum? Ruby, you have gum in your hair?" Maude asked.

"No, but you do," Ruby replied directly.

Maude's face turned a slight shade of pink, before then turning bright red. "Let me get this straight. First, Opal drugs me in an airport. Then she gives me gum. Then the gum ends up in my hair. And you're all just telling me this so calmly?"

Before either of them could answer, she ran her fingers through her hair and finally found the wad of dried gum near the back of her head. "Ugh!"

"It isn't the first time you've been drugged, nor will it be the last," Opal shrugged. "And Ruby, you know you were well past tired of hearing her complain. Did you really want to sit on an airplane next to her for hours while she complained? No. No you did not."

"I didn't think you would drug her!" Ruby said.

"You're blowing that word out of proportion," Opal said. She turned to Maude and continued. "It's not a drug. It's pure lavender, mixed with chamomile tea, and valerian root oil. It's been studied for ages and I can hardly keep it in stock at the store. And as for gum, this cream will get it out. Or I can always cut it once we get back home."

"I'm never, and I mean never ever drinking or eating anything you touch. Ever. Again," Maude screeched. She grabbed the handles of her two suitcases and marched towards the car parking garage.

"You said so yourself that you felt well rested!" Opal shouted after her.

"You shouldn't have done that, Opal," Ruby said disapprovingly. "I would never do something like that."

"Oh hush, Ruby. I'd do it again in a heartbeat. Stop being all holier than thou," Opal sassed. She grabbed her luggage and hurriedly followed after Maude.

Opal had never sassed Ruby before. She wasn't quite sure how to take it. On one hand, Opal had been right. They were both tired of hearing Maude complain about everything. Especially when it came to flying. On the other hand, Opal had basically drugged Maude without her knowing. Opal was very skilled with all of her natural products, so Ruby wasn't really worried that it would affect her health or anything. Maude needed to be taken down a few notches, but there needed to be a line. She knew that Maude would never have willingly taken anything prescribed by Opal, and she had to admit that besides the snoring, the complaint-free flight had been nice.

"Oh heavens, they've really left me here!" Ruby said frantically. She grabbed her two suitcases and purse and pushed her way through the crowd to chase after Maude and Opal.

She finally found them by the car waiting for her. It was a quiet drive out of the airport parking garage. Opal turned on the radio to a low volume and quietly hummed along. After about thirty minutes on the road, Maude cleared her throat from the backseat.

"I could still use a good coffee," she said quietly.

Opal grinned and found a good exit. Gas station coffee was not the preferred coffee, but it would do. She waited in the car while Ruby and Maude went inside to potty and shop for snacks. She looked down at the gas gauge and realized that they desperately needed gas if they wanted to make it all the way back home. She backed into a spot near one of the gas pumps and got out to fill up the tank.

As she was finishing, Ruby and Maude exited the gas station and walked back to the car. They each had a bag full of snacks and a cup of coffee in hand. Ruby handed Opal a bottle of water and a bag of hard candy.

"Here you go, you old coot," Maude sighed. She handed Opal a package of oatmeal raisin cookies and glared at her.

"Thank you both," Opal laughed. "I knew you couldn't stay mad at me. Especially when I have the keys." She hopped back into the car and revved the engine loudly. "All aboard!" she yelled loudly and honked the horn for good measure.

The rest of the drive back to Rhinestone was lively. They found a classic country radio station and sang along to every song that played. When a Marty Robbins classic faded out, Opal began to laugh.

"Did I ever tell y'all what happened to Mortie last month?" Opal asked.

"No," Ruby said slowly. She wasn't sure she wanted to know what the local funeral director who doubled as the county coroner had gotten into. Nor was she sure how the story could relate to what they had just been listening to.

"Oh, it's a doozy," Opal said.

Ruby looked behind her at Maude who shrugged. "Well, go on and tell us," Maude said.

"I know y'all heard about Roy's cousin Lester over in Montgomery. The one who got struck by lightning?" Opal explained.

"I did hear about that!" Ruby said. "It was so awful."

"Wait a minute," Maude said. "Wasn't he the one who was naked except for the clamps on his, well, his nipples? He was standing out there in the middle of the yard in the thunderstorm! Y'all!"

"That was him," Opal nodded. She caught Ruby's wide-eyed stare and chuckled. "They didn't release all that to the public."

"Goodness!" Ruby exclaimed.

"Well, the story gets even more interesting," Opal said.

"How can it?" Ruby gasped.

"It's Rhinestone," Maude said. "Anything is possible."

"But this wasn't in Rhinestone," Ruby pointed out.

"The next part is," Opal said. "Anyway, Mortie drove up and picked up the body and brought it back to Ravens because Roy and them didn't want to deal with all the hullabaloo up there. Well, I won't go into details, but it couldn't be an open casket, let's just say."

"I can't imagine why," Maude rolled her eyes.

"So, the family opted for cremation. Usually Mortie places the body in a sheet, but the family requested that Lester wear his favorite pair of coveralls for the cremation," Opal continued.

"That's not strange," Ruby said.

"Lester was a farmer," Opal said. "He had two hundred acres of corn."

"There's a lot of corn farmers in our area," Ruby shrugged. "I don't see why this is the strange part of the story."

Opal looked in the rear-view mirror and shook her head. "I guess Lester must have had a habit of eating raw corn. Anyway, his favorite pair of coveralls had been stuffed with corn kernels."

"Oh my God," Maude howled. "Corn kernels! No!"

Ruby turned and looked at Opal slowly. "Opal, no! That poor man!"

"Well, he was already passed, Ruby. But it near about scared Mortie to death. He said he never in all his years heard such a racket. Sounded like gunshots or fireworks going off. Near about blew the roof off the oven," Opal said. "That didn't make the news either."

"That can't be real!" Maude laughed. "Popcorn at the crematorium!"

"I wouldn't eat that popcorn," Opal said seriously.

"This is not appropriate!" Ruby squealed. "Y'all! That is awful."

"I've always said that the mortuary business isn't for the faint of heart," Opal said.

"That's for sure," Maude laughed again. "Oh goodness!"

"How did we get on this subject?" Ruby asked once Maude had calmed down.

"We passed a cornfield a ways back and it made me think of it," Opal explained.

"So awful," Ruby repeated.

"That's how I'd want to go out," Opal mused. "With a bang."

"Or, in his case, a pop," Maude added.

"Y'all quit! God rest his poor soul," Ruby lamented. "Can we please change the subject?"

"We sure can, Rubes," Opal nodded. "Maude, when can I fix your hair?"

"I had forgotten about that," Maude grimaced. "I guess sometime tomorrow."

"Don't forget we have our ladies auxiliary meeting tomorrow afternoon," Ruby reminded them.

"That's right," Opal agreed. "Have either of you thought more about what you want to include in the time capsule?"

"I think I'm going to put a pressed magnolia flower in there," Ruby said. "I hope long after I'm gone that the Manor will still be thriving. Between Mavis and Wilbur, I'm sure it will be."

"I love that," Opal said. "I'm going to include some salves and maybe a vial of that sleep aid," she laughed. "What about you, Maude?"

"I've been thinking of a few things," she nodded. "Maybe one of my granddad's wrenches. He opened the first mechanic shop in Rhinestone over sixty years ago. I've got one more thing in mind, but I may keep it as a surprise for now."

Opal and Ruby looked at each other, but merely shrugged. When Opal pulled into her driveway a few minutes later, the sun was just beginning to set behind the clouds.

"Well, another fun adventure as the Stone Sisters," Opal smiled. "I'll make sure I update the old bucket list."

"Definitely," Ruby nodded. She helped them maneuver their suitcases and bags out of the trunk and backseat.

"Don't forget that you packed some stuff in my bag," Opal said to Ruby. "Want to come inside and figure out what we need to separate?"

"I packed some shoes and two sweaters in there," Ruby said. "I can get them from you tomorrow or another day after that. I'm not worried about them."

"Well, be careful driving home. I know you're excited to see your crew. Tell them we said hello and we'll see them tomorrow," Maude said.

"And we won't tell them about my adventure at the concert," Ruby reminded them.

"Of course, Ruby," Opal chuckled. She winked at Maude and waved goodbye as Maude drug her luggage towards her house and Ruby climbed into her car to drive home.

It didn't take her long to get to Magnolia Manor. As soon as she pulled up, Mavis busted out the front door and ran to give her a big hug. Jameson and Wilbur followed not far behind her.

"You're back!" Mavis shrieked!

Round Trip

After many rounds of hugs, Jameson and Wilbur gathered Ruby's bags and followed her and Mavis up the steps and into the house.

"We saved you a plate, Big Mama!" Wilbur said. He pointed to a Styrofoam container on the stove. "Mavis wanted to eat at the Big Steer, so we brought you some steak, a baked potato, and some carrot soufflé."

"Thank you, honey! That's exactly what I wanted," Ruby grinned. "But first, I have gifts for everyone!"

"Yay!" Mavis clapped. "I love gifts!"

They all gathered in the living room a few minutes later for Ruby to present her trinkets and souvenirs. She found the bag of shirts first and handed them out. For Jameson, she got a black sweatshirt that had the Empire State Building on it. Wilbur and Mavis each received a black sweatshirt with the Statue of Liberty emblazoned across the chest. They each received a white short-sleeve shirt with the words I Love NY across the top with a bright red heart.

Wilbur unwrapped a snow globe with a miniature Statue of Liberty in the center, while Mavis cuddled her teddy bear that wore a shirt that said New York City across it. Jameson loved his mug from Ellen's Stardust Diner and vowed to take it to the office on Monday.

Ruby showed them the postcards, stamps, and brochures that she had collected from around the city. Even though she had called home every evening while she was away, she still had so much to tell them about. They moved to the kitchen where she continued to answer their questions while she ate her supper. They couldn't wait to see the photographs once they were developed.

Later that evening, after Wilbur and Mavis went to bed, Ruby told Jameson all about their adventure at the drag club. Jameson roared with laughter and found it hilarious that Ruby had gotten accidentally snockered.

"I wish I could have been a fly on that wall," he laughed. "Those are the pictures I can't wait to see!"

"They better not have taken any photographs there!" Ruby said. But she was certain that Maude, and definitely Opal, had to have taken at least a few.

As they got ready for bed that night, Ruby sat on the edge of the bed and asked Jameson what they had all been up to this past week.

"Well, Wilbur and I have been having a little adventure in the evenings," he said. "Mavis started out helping, but she got bored, I reckon."

Ruby took off her slippers and tucked them under the bed, waiting for him to go on.

"You see, we couldn't just walk away from it. It was too good of a deal," he continued.

"I'm almost afraid to ask," Ruby said.

"One of my clients had it for sale, so Wilbur and I went over there Monday evening, and we hailed it home."

Ruby saw the childlike grin slowly spread across his face.

"Mavis fell in love with it! Now, it needs a new motor and we had to build a wider roll cage for it, but every kid needs a go-kart," he smiled.

Chapter Twenty

After church the next day, Mavis couldn't wait to show Ruby her new go-kart. The paint was flaking off of the base and the seat had a rip across the center. It had quite a bit of wear and tear on it, but Jameson assured Ruby that it was safe. He and Wilbur had spent hours each evening making sure it would run.

Watching Mavis zip back-and-forth across the yard on it was well worth the money it took to fix it up. Jameson and Ruby sat on the porch in the rocking chairs while Wilbur read a book in the swing.

"Honey, don't you want to ride with Mavis on that contraption?" Ruby asked Wilbur.

"Oh, no ma'am! I made that mistake yesterday," he laughed. "I like my two feet on the ground."

"And I like my feet up here on the porch," Jameson added. "Mavis has already run over my feet twice!"

Wilbur grinned behind his book and peeked over the top of it to watch Mavis run over a pile of sticks near the barn.

"Sugar, be careful over there!" Jameson called out, but Mavis didn't hear him.

Over the noise of Mavis' go-kart, they didn't hear Maude and Opal trekking up the driveway a few minutes later in Opal's small car. Opal honked the horn twice and had to slam on brakes to avoid Mavis' reckless driving on her way to park next to the signature magnolia tree.

"Maybe she needs another lesson on driving," Wilbur chuckled. "She's a little all over the place."

"You just succinctly described Mavis' whole personality," Jameson agreed. He stood up and wiped his glasses with his handkerchief, hugged Ruby, and walked down the steps to try and corral Mavis.

"Be careful, Wilbur. You don't need her to run over any part of you," Ruby said. "Remember that I have a big pot of soup on the stove, so please keep an eye on it in case Mavis takes out Jameson." She hugged him goodbye and walked down the steps towards Opal's car.

Once Ruby was inside the car, Opal checked multiple times before she backed out of the driveway.

"I see Mavis has a new toy," Maude said. "She near about took us out a minute ago."

"She never has learned the word careful," Ruby said. "Jameson bought it for her while I was gone. He and Wilbur built a new roll cage for it, and now I see why."

"She sure keeps you young!" Opal laughed. "Did she like her gifts?"

"Oh yes!" Ruby nodded. "They all did. And I told Jameson about your little mix up, Maude. He says if there are any photos from that night, and I told him there better not be, that he would pay big money to see them."

Opal and Maude both started to laugh, which confirmed Ruby's suspicions that there was indeed photographic evidence of her drunken night on the town.

"If y'all show anyone those, I'll kill you," Ruby swore. "I swear you two are double trouble."

"Sure, Ruby, sure," Opal winked in the rear-view mirror. "Did you tell him about our portrait we had drawn?"

"I told him you'd bring it over one evening for him to see. I'm not sure the kids need to view it," Ruby laughed.

"Can't imagine why," Maude said.

The Ladies Auxiliary had planned to meet that afternoon in the banquet room of City Hall with the mayor, city council, the local principal, and the head of the PTO from the school. Together they were all going to go over the list of items for the time capsule.

Opal pulled into the parking lot next to a bright red convertible that they all knew well.

"What's Nadine doing here?" Opal asked. "I thought she wasn't flying in til this afternoon?"

"She must have caught an earlier flight," Ruby suggested.

Maude shrugged and looked inside the car that had the roof down. She thought about ripping open the bag of bird seed that she and Opal had just picked up from the hardware store and dumping it all over Nadine's car, but decided to try Ruby's advice and be the bigger person. Ruby was right, they did seem to be in a good place at the moment anyway.

"Come on, Maude. Looks like we're the last ones here," Opal called over her shoulder. She and Ruby were already at the front entrance waiting for her.

"Hold your horses! I'm coming," she huffed.

Inside they found everyone snacking and talking around a long table. The table was full of water bottles and soda cans, a fruit tray, and small chocolate chip cookies.

"There they are!" Mayor Humperdink announced. "Nadine was just regaling us with some of your big city adventures."

"Oh, was she?" squeaked Maude. "Don't believe everything you hear."

"I thought your flight was later this evening," Ruby asked Nadine.

"I called Martin yesterday and had him switch me to an earlier flight this morning. I drove straight here from Atlanta. There was no way I would miss this meeting," Nadine smiled.

"Of course," Maude sighed.

"We are so glad you are all back home!" the mayor smiled. "Nadine was telling us about your eating competition. I must say, that sounds interesting."

"It was nothing," Maude tried to say convincingly.

"Oh Maude, don't be shy. I was just telling them how you bested all those men in that cannoli eating competition," Nadine smiled.

"That is true," Opal nodded. "They weren't even close to her new record!"

"It wasn't something we could ever host here in Rhinestone. We are, well, most of us, are too refined and well-mannered for that kind of thing," Nadine smiled. "But then there's Maude. She showed those potbellied men how it was done."

"She destroyed them!" echoed Opal.

"How interesting!" the mayor said again. "I'm glad you were all able to experience that together.

"That wasn't all. Maude, tell them how you almost got kicked out of heaven," Nadine continued.

"What?" the crowd gasped.

"What? Heaven?" Maude asked.

"It was not for the faint of heart," Nadine said. "There was this wooden roller coaster that Maude was set on going on. No one wanted to ride with her, so I asked a sweet young lady to accompany her, and the sweet sister was subjected to near torture."

"I didn't know you had a sister, Maude!" Sue exclaimed.

"Oh God no," Maude replied.

"A rea sister," Nadine explained. "A nun sister."

"Oh," Sue nodded. "That makes more sense."

"Yes, Maude showed out like her usual self and once the ride was over, she got set upon by some nuns and a Catholic priest," Nadine explained. She turned towards Maude and playfully slapped her knee. "That's about as close to heaven as you may get," she laughed.

"Now Nadine, it wasn't like that," Ruby interrupted.

"Well, it kind of was," Opal mused.

"Well, yes, but they thought she was possessed by demons," Ruby explained.

"Maude's temper was certainly something else," Nadine reiterated.

"But they forgave her, so her soul should be fine," Opal shrugged.

"I don't think it works that way," Pastor Miles said, but no one was listening.

"Well, at any rate, we are so glad that you are all back in one piece from your trip," Mayor Humperdink said. "Let's um, let's all gather around and see what all we have that's being donated thus far."

He picked up the clipboard from the table in front of him and began to read aloud. "So far we have a graduation cord donated by the school, a signed copy of Rhinestone Recipes, a copy of the original charter, this week's Rhinestone Register, and a postcard of the river junction. Oh, and the mayor from Junction has donated a beautiful hand drawn picture of the Rhinestone chamber. He's a very gifted artist, on top of being the second-best mayor our county has," he chuckled. "Anyway, we're going to go around the room now and suggest some other items. So, who would like to start?"

Opal raised her hand and stepped forward regally. "I'd like to include some of my all-natural products from my Color Me Crazy line." Her suggestion was met with nods and cheers from the women. "The all-natural healing properties come from our very land here in Rhinestone. The history of Rhinestone shines so bright from the people who want nothing more than to live in harmony and peace with each other, now and forever."

She gave a low bow and was met with a thunderous applause. Opal was ever the entertainer.

"I'd like to include a pressed magnolia from the tree in my front yard. That tree has weathered a lot over its many decades, just like our town. It, like Rhinestone, is strong and has had to adapt as time goes on. Plus, that land has been in Jameson's family since the very beginning of Rhinestone," Ruby offered.

She too was met with immediate nods of agreement.

"How beautiful! Personal items that mean so much to the community," Nadine smiled sweetly. "I love how giving we all are! That is the spirit, my friends!"

"I'd like to include a wrench from the original Coop's Tire. My grandfather started one of the first businesses here in Rhinestone, and it's still in the family today with my great-nephew running it. I'd also like to nominate a donation from our goodwill ambassador herself, Nadine Waters," Maude began.

"Oh," Nadine smiled. "And what would you like to suggest that I donate?"

"Well, I thought since you are the first and foremost Miss Rhinestone, that it would only be fitting for us to commemorate the occasion by donating an actual piece of history," Maude explained.

Nadine's eyes lit up at the mention of her pageant title. "What are you suggesting?" she asked.

"Your tiara, of course," Maude said.

Nadine's jaw dropped, but Maude's suggestion was met with applause. The mayor clapped Nadine on the back and thanked her for her donation. "The future of Rhinestone will know without a doubt that Rhinestone was built on a firm foundation of strength, intellect, and beauty."

"My tiara?" Nadine whispered.

"Yes, the original Miss Rhinestone tiara. I don't imagine we have room for the fabric strip thing, but whatever you think," Maude said.

"It's a sash," Nadine snapped.

"Whatever," Maude smiled.

Ruby and Opal stood stone faced next to Maude watching the interaction.

"What do you say, Nadine?" the mayor asked.

Nadine braced herself against the table and smiled sweetly. "Of course I will put my tiara in the time capsule. I'll even xerox a copy of the newspaper article detailing how I won. Maude, I'm afraid that your name isn't mentioned at all, but those who come in last place rarely are."

"Ah, yes. Well, thank you, Nadine. That is very honorable of you. Alright, who is next?" Mayor Humperdink said.

"I was thinking of maybe putting in one of the scraps of original wallpaper from the vestibule of Beaver Crossing Holy Church," Sue offered.

"Great idea," the group agreed.

They continued to toss around ideas as a group. The tension in the room between Maude and Nadine was palpable. When the mayor finally dismissed the group, after they finalized the potluck plans, everyone said their quick goodbyes and filtered out.

Ruby followed behind Opal and Maude to the parking lot. "Maude, I'm surprised at you! I thought you two had finally put all this drama behind you and you do and do something like that!" Ruby sighed.

"She told everyone I had been kicked out of heaven!" Maude sneered.

"Who cares what she says?" Ruby exclaimed. "And she certainly doesn't have any authority over who gets into heaven or not. Seriously Maude, I thought you were more mature than that."

"Well, there's your first mistake, Ruby," Opal laughed.

Maude cut her eyes at Opal and yanked on the door handle of Opal's car. Opal reached over and unlocked the passenger door for Maude to slide inside. Once Ruby was settled in the backseat, Opal started the car and looked around before backing out of the parking lot.

Nadine was already long gone. She was one of the first people to leave once the meeting was dismissed. Ruby, Maude, and Opal stayed behind to help take out the trash and wipe down the tables.

"Well, all I'm saying is that you need to make things right," Ruby sighed again from the backseat.

In an effort to change the subject, Opal asked what was on the supper menu at Magnolia Manor.

"I made my mother's baked potato soup recipe. It's been simmering all afternoon. We picked up some bread from the Piggly Wiggly after church to go with it. I made plenty, so if y'all want any, come on," Ruby answered.

"I won't say no," Opal smiled. "I have your shoes and sweaters in the trunk, too. What about you, you old bird?"

Maude rolled her eyes at Opal's comment, but nodded in agreement. "Let's stop by the Pig on the way to Ruby's. I'll get us a lemon pound cake and some ice cream to go with supper. You know dessert's my favorite part of any meal anyway."

"You don't say," Opal laughed sarcastically. "You know, I learn something new about you every day."

"Oh hush," Maude rolled her eyes.

Opal pulled into one of the empty spots near the front entrance of the Piggly Wiggly. She and Ruby sat in the car while Maude went inside to shop.

"You think she'll be ok in there without supervision?" Opal asked.

"Probably not," Ruby laughed. "I wonder what all she will come out with."

Twenty minutes later, Maude exited the grocery store with half of a cart full. Opal shook her head as she got closer and hopped out of the front seat to help her unload her cart into the trunk.

"How much toilet paper do you go through?" Opal asked.

"It was on sale," Maude shrugged.

"And was it three cakes for the price of one?" Opal asked.

"No," Maude stuck her tongue out. "I couldn't decide between the lemon, the chocolate, or the plain one. So I had to get three different ice creams, too." She held up the cartons of vanilla, chocolate, and strawberry ice cream.

"Obviously," Opal nodded. "And air freshener. Well, I know why you need that. And dog food, of course. But what in the world is this?"

"I saw it in the produce section by the kiwis," Maude shrugged.

"But what is it?" Opal asked.

"I don't know. It looks like one of those weird fruit things that you'd like to try," Maude said.

"Is it some kind of dragon fruit?" Opal asked. She held it up towards the sun to get a better look at it.

"How in the hell would I know?" Maude asked. "I don't eat regular fruits, let alone those fairytale ones you talk about."

"I'll cut into it at Ruby's. Thanks!" Opal smiled.

Mavis was still zipping around the yard when the women pulled into the driveway. They could see Wilbur in the barn playing with the barn cats while Jameson was still on the porch carving a block of wood.

"I'm a little surprised that Jameson's letting her tear up the yard like that," Maude said.

"Grandkids will change you," Ruby smiled.

༶Chapter Twenty-One༶

On the following Saturday, the Montgomery family piled into their car and drove to the town square along with every other family in rhinestone to the centennial celebration.

The afternoon kicked off with a large-scale cookout. Everyone had been asked to bring a dessert or covered dish to share. The city council donated the paper products and the local butcher shop provided the hotdogs and hamburgers cooked on one of their massive grills.

The main event of the celebration was the time capsule. At three o'clock in the afternoon, the time capsule would be filled, and then sealed, before being buried right there in the center of the field next to the chamber offices.

Many local vendors had set up booths and tents to showcase and sell their products. Local farmers had their products laid out next to basket weavers, furniture makers, and other local craftsmen.

A dog and cat rescue from Junction had set up an adoption event with some of their rescue animals hoping for a new home. Eddie Walker and his new fiancée handed out flowers to everyone who passed by. Local newspapers and news stations from around the tri-county area had sent out their reporters in full force. It was a wonderful turnout and a beautiful day for such an epic celebration.

When they arrived downtown, Jameson carried the tray of cookies that Ruby had baked in one hand and the pan of chocolate delight in the other.

Mavis had never seen so much food in her entire life. There had to be at least fifteen large picnic tables, each with a red and white checkered plastic tablecloth on top. Each picnic table was covered with dishes and pans and Tupperware in every color.

One table was piled high with hotdog and hamburger buns next to large platters full of smoking hamburgers and freshly grilled hotdogs. Bottles of ketchup, mustard, and jars of pickles were scattered about the table. Plates stacked high with yellow cheese, lettuce, and tomatoes were in between the platters of meat. The next table was piled high with paper plates, napkins, utensils, and plastic cups. There were three tables with water bottles, soda cans, pitchers of lemonade, and jugs of what had to be homemade sweet tea. One table they passed had bags of chips and small packages of salted peanuts scattered across the top. All of those tables made her mouth water, but then she saw the dessert tables.

Four of the longest picnic tables were covered in every single kind of dessert that she could think of. There were lemon bars, chocolate layered cakes, butter pound cakes, strawberry cupcakes with pink sprinkles, cookies of all shapes and sizes and flavors, and piles of homemade fudge. Chocolate brownies with walnuts and homemade blondies with butterscotch chips were next to the edge. Mavis' hand crept towards the plastic wrap, but Jameson smiled and told her she needed to wait until it was time to eat. He made room in the center of one of the tables for Ruby's pan of chocolate delight and tray of cookies.

"Look at that table over yonder! Those pies look good!" he said. "I'm going to make sure to save some room for a slice."

There was every kind of pie that you could think of, even four large apple pies with a lattice worked crust. Mavis hurriedly looked around for cartons of ice cream and was disappointed when she didn't see any. How could anyone expect her to eat apple pie without a big scoop of vanilla ice cream on top?

She began to aimlessly walk towards the table with the pies, but Wilbur steered her attention back towards Ruby and Jameson who were now spreading a large blanket on the ground not far from the dessert tables. Maude and Opal had saved them a spot underneath one of the giant live oak trees next to their smaller blankets.

"Anyone going to join us?" Jameson asked.

"Not that I know of," Opal sighed. "Mortie's over there at the table with the council and other high-ranking officials. He's so important. He said he would have to be on high alert today. Near about everyone in town is going to be here, so the odds of someone dropping dead are quite high."

"Thank you for that, Opal," Jameson laughed.

"Opal! Not in front of the kids," Ruby whispered.

Wilbur chuckled and looked at Mavis whose attention had already drifted back towards the tables full of desserts.

"Well, it's true," Opal said. "It's pure psychology. You can't get a big group of people together without something going haywire."

"As long as there's no thunderstorm or corn kernels, we should be fine," Maude interjected.

"Y'all, stop," Ruby chastised. "I can't hear what they're saying up there on the stage. Can you?"

"Looks like the Preacher just blessed the food, so let's go get in line," Jameson suggested. "I've got to eat quickly so I can help Lucien and Frank wheel the time capsule over from the bank vault. The joker is heavier than it looks."

"How are they going to bury it once it's full?" Wilbur asked.

"Frank's already dug the hole with his new backhoe. Soon as we get it full of the town's treasure and sealed, we will get it in the hole and he'll cover it with the dirt that he's already dug up," Jameson explained. "At least, that's the plan," he winked.

"Do you think he'd let me take a look at it?" Wilbur asked. "At his new backhoe?"

"I don't see why not! How about you walk over with me after we eat and we'll take a look at it," Jameson offered.

Wilbur's smile lit up like fireworks in the night sky. He loved farm machinery and tried to learn more about it every chance he got. Ruby wouldn't be surprised if Magnolia Manor ended up buying a backhoe within the next few weeks. Jameson had an obsession with farm equipment and a soft spot when it came to passing along those traditions and collections down to future generations.

"Now let's see what we've got here," Jameson said. He stood over the first table and read the labels on the jugs and pitchers before pouring sweet tea for Mavis and Wilbur. "I think I'll sample some of this lemonade." He took a big sip of the yellow liquid and pursed his lips instantly. His eyes all but crossed.

"That sure is something," he whispered. "I love lemon, but that is pure sour. I think I'll stick with the sweet tea after all."

They all piled their plates with hotdogs and hamburgers and chips. Ruby promised Mavis she could have her pick of a dessert or two as soon as she ate her two hotdogs. The adults and Wilbur balanced their plates on their laps, but Mavis sprawled out across the blanket on her stomach and began to eat ravenously.

Opal pulled a wrapped sandwich out of her purse once she sat down on her blanket and took a drink from her metal water bottle that she had brought with her.

"You brought your own food to a town picnic?" Maude asked.

Suddenly it dawned on Ruby. "I didn't even think about that when we planned the menu!" Ruby gasped. "I'm so sorry, Opal."

"No worries. Just because I don't eat meat doesn't mean anyone else should go without the staple of all good southern picnics," Opal smiled.

"What did you bring, Ms. Opal?" Mavis asked.

"I brought Maude's favorite, a jello salad, to share with everyone. But for me, I packed a sandwich," she smiled. "Nothing beats a mayonnaise and tomato sandwich. I made my own rosemary mayonnaise yesterday with the rosemary from my herb garden. Want a bite?"

"No thanks," Mavis frowned. She licked the salt from the potato chips off her fingers and then wiped her fingers on her shorts for good measure.

When they had all finished their lunch, it was finally time for dessert. They all sampled quite a few different desserts from the tables and talked about their favorites.

"I know you two have your differences, Maude, but Nadine's lemon squares are sinful," Jameson said. He popped another whole square into his mouth and savored it. "Not as good as your tea cakes of course," he winked at Ruby.

Ruby blushed and shook her head. "You two get on out of here," she motioned towards him and Wilbur. "We'll head that way in a few minutes or so to get a good view of the capsule."

Wilbur nodded and wrapped two of Ruby's famous cookies in his napkin and put them in his front shirt pocket for safe keeping. Her tea cakes were one of his favorite foods on earth. No one made them quite like Big Mama Ruby did.

"They are good," Opal said to Maude after Jameson and Wilbur had walked away. "You'd like them if you'd get off your high horse and try one."

Maude rolled her eyes and dug her fork into the piece of chocolate sheet cake on her plate.

"I can get you one, Ms. Maude," Mavis perked up. "I've already eaten my cookies and piece of pie. I need to try one of those strawberry cupcakes."

"No thank you," Maude smiled warmly. "Let's go get you a cupcake though."

She followed Mavis to the table with cupcakes and helped the little girl pick out the best one. She caught a glimpse of Nadine from across the field talking to the mayor. She glanced at the picnic table and saw two lemon squares left.

"Oh, fine!" she huffed, and snatched one of them from the platter. She took a small bite, expecting to hate it and spit it back into the napkin. To her surprise, the morsel melted in her mouth. She ate the rest of the treat in one bite. After looking around to make sure that no one else was looking, she quickly grabbed the remaining lemon square and shoved it into her mouth. As annoying as she was, Jameson and Opal had been right. Nadine's lemon squares were like manna from heaven.

After Mavis was satisfied with her dessert intake, the ladies shook off the blankets and folded them up.

Maude carried them back to her car and threw them in her trunk before joining them all back near the town square where the time capsule was waiting. The mayor had a picnic table full of treasures that had been agreed upon for the time capsule. Ruby's pressed magnolia flower was sealed in a plastic bag, and Opal's salve and cream collection were tied together with twine. Each treasure had a tag attached to it detailing what it was and who had generously donated it.

Nadine, as the representative for the Ladies Auxiliary Club, stood on the makeshift stage along with the mayor and the members of the city council. The town watched in awe as Principal Harvey and PTO members carefully laid each of the donated treasures into the time capsule.

After every item had been placed inside, Nadine laid a bouquet of red roses on the top of the pile and nodded. Pastor Miles of Beaver Crossing Holy Church for the Faithful came to the stage and set a prayer for the future generations of rhinestone.

A group of men slowly pushed the lid of the time capsule into place and hammered it along the edges to make sure that it had sealed. Once it was deemed perfect, Jameson cleared the area and Frank Jones used his backhoe to edge the time capsule gently into the hole that he had previously dug for it. The crowd cheered as he pushed the dirt back into place with the giant machine. Wilbur, Jameson, and Mayor Humperdink each took a shovel and patted the ground level on top of the raised mound.

"Over the next few days, a white fence will be erected around the buried capsule, after the concrete block is placed on top, of course," Mayor Humperdink said. "We have left strict instructions to the mayor and council of Rhinestone in the year 2039 for the opening of the capsule. Yes, it was originally one hundred years, but quite a few concerns were raised about that. None of us will be around in one hundred years, though I dare say that many of us will be around in fifty," the mayor smiled. He posed for another picture and then thanked everyone for making the centennial celebration a certified hit. He encouraged everyone to continue to enjoy the afternoon out in the town square and to make sure that everyone cleaned up after themselves.

"I reckon it's time for a nap," Jameson yawned.

"Now that I can agree with," Maude said. "Buford whined all night and I barely got any sleep."

"He wants a friend," Opal said sagely.

"He's got a friend. I'm his friend and I'm the only friend he needs," Maude said sourly.

"He needs a dog friend that doesn't snore so loudly at night," Opal whispered to Mavis. "How you and me go over to the adoption booth and find Maude another new friend?"

"Ms. Maude is getting a new puppy!" Mavis squealed.

"What? I already have a new puppy," Maude retorted. "One is more than enough."

"I'm with Mavis," Opal agreed. "Buford needs a sweet puppy friend to tire him out during the day while you nap. You'll have to come up with another day because you can't have two Buford's at the same time. Come on, Maude, it can't hurt to look. The dog shelter from Junction brought a whole pack over. I walked by them earlier and there were only a few left for adoption."

"I don't know about this," Maude said.

"There were plenty of cats left," Opal pointed out.

"I think I'd rather have the dog," Maude said quickly.

"Then it's settled!" Opal smiled.

"Oh! We must go look, Ms. Maude!" Mavis squealed.

"Well, it sounds like the rest of your afternoon is booked!" Jameson winked at Ruby. "You know, it wouldn't be so bad having a dog around the place."

Wilbur snapped to attention. "A dog?" he whispered.

"Have you ever had a dog?" Mavis asked him.

Wilbur shook his head.

"Can we get one, Big Daddy? Big Mama?" Mavis pleaded. "Wilbur's never had a dog of his own and I think he's big enough. I can help him watch the dog. I know we'd both be very good with a dog. Right, Wilbur? You think you're big enough?" she asked Wilbur.

Wilbur broke out into a grin and patted Mavis on the back.

"Well, Wilbur?" Jameson asked. He too had a childlike grin on his face.

"Yes sir, I think I'm big enough," Wilbur chuckled.

Mavis jumped into Jameson's arm and wrapped her arms around his neck. "I always wanted a dog! And Wilbur has, too! Come on Big Daddy! Let's get me a dog, and Wilbur a dog, and Ms. Maude a dog. You want one, too, Ms. Opal?"

"Oh heavens," Ruby exclaimed. "What have you started?" she asked Jameson.

Acknowledgments

We would never have been able to finish this book, or any of the others, without the love and support of our families and friends. To our loved ones, once again we hope we haven't embarrassed you too much with this next installment of the Magnolia Manor series. We had so much fun talking about the Big Apple in this book! Anytime that Ruby, Maude, and Opal have the opportunity to travel, hilarity is sure to ensue.

We'd like to thank the ladies at Southern Willow Publishing. Jaimie, Jennifer, and Victoria continue to believe in us and support our adventurous tales. It is due to their professionalism and experiences that we have been able to publish our sixth novel in the series.

Round Trip

We look forward to many more adventures ahead with the Rhinestone gang.

About the Authors

Wanda Jennings and Louise Turner have known each other since they were young(er). They began their writing careers later in life after retiring from their professional careers in civil service and social work.

When not writing the Magnolia Manor series, Louise and Wanda enjoy traveling, playing board games, and trying new food.

Dear Reader,

We hope you enjoyed *Round Trip*. We are truly blessed that you took the time (again) to spend a few hours with some of our favorite members of the Rhinestone gang. Rhinestone has a wonderful collection of true characters, that's for sure! It's hard to not fall in love with them over and over again.

We are currently working on the next book in the Magnolia Manor series that will be out at the end of 2022. This next book takes place during the fall of 2021, where we see the return of Earl Thibodeaux Boudreaux at Rhinestone's annual county fair.

If you enjoyed *Dirty Laundry, Saints & Sinners, Color Me Crazy, Double Trouble, Now & Forever,* and *Round Trip*, please make sure to join us on our next adventure in *Hold Your Horses!* Thank you again for reading *Round Trip*. We would really appreciate it if you could take a few minutes and leave us a positive review on Amazon.com and Goodreads.com. Your feedback is very important to us and it helps spread the word about our series. Join us on Facebook (@LouiseandWanda) to keep up with all of our adventures. We also got an Instagram so we can keep up with the younger crowd! We love to interact with our fans!

Thank you again for humoring two old ladies. We always wanted to share the Rhinestone gang with the world, and we are so thankful that we found a way to do it. Make sure you tell your friends about this series so they too can fall in love with our gang. We look forward to a long line of books in this series.

Love,

Louise & Wanda

Books in the Magnolia Manor Series

Dirty Laundry

Saints & Sinners

Color Me Crazy

Double Trouble

Now and Forever

Round Trip

Hold Your Horses (Due Winter 2022!)

The adventures will continue next summer. Join Opal, Maude, Ruby, and the whole Rhinestone gang in

Hold Your Horses

Available Winter of 2022!